A HANDSOME STRANGER, A TERRIFYING MONSTER, A BOY WHO BURNS AND BURNS…

"*The Devil in Midwinter* is a beautiful tapestry of myth and legend and love, woven into a small town romance."

—Amalia Dillin, author of *Forged by Fate*

"A mash-up of Mexican folklore and the classic Sleeping Beauty, set in the orchards of Washington, *The Devil In Midwinter* is a stunning romance that put me in mind of the lush works of Charles De Lint."

—Kristina Wojtaszek, author of *Opal*

The Devil in Midwinter

ELISE FORIER EDIE

World Weaver Press

THE DEVIL IN MIDWINTER

This is a work of fiction; characters and events are either fictitious or used fictitiously.

Published by World Weaver Press
Alpena, Michigan
www.WorldWeaverPress.com

Edited by Eileen Wiedbrauk
Cover designed by World Weaver Press

First Novella Edition: April 2014
Originally published in *A Winter's Enchantment* December 2013

ISBN: 0615990002
ISBN-13: 978-0615990002

Also available as an ebook.

To Keith and Vivi

ACKNOWLEDGMENTS

The Devil in Midwinter would never have happened if my husband Keith and my daughter Genevieve hadn't let me spend an entire Christmas break holed up in my room, writing like mad. Thank you very much, you guys. You are terrific at supporting my dreams.

Thanks to my Mattawa family, Joyce and Keith, to the Lion's Club and Hot Desert Nights, to the Fireman's Ball, to Big Cups Coffee and La Popular, The Mattawa Area News, the Millbrandt vineyard, Big Fork Orchards and the fantastic school kids and teachers at the Wahluke School District. You might not know it, but every one of you inspired me in a hundred little ways.

Thank you to dogs everywhere, but especially my dogs, who appear in this book disguised as three Great Pyrenees.

Special thanks to my writing group, Robin, Carolyn and Maria, and to Kathy, who held my hand through every recent artistic process.

And finally, wherever you are Sarah Breedin, you who dared to have a Harlequin Romance book subscription in high school, and unapologetically devoured trashy novels by the dozen, thanks for cheerfully lending me all those books back in the day, when I was over at your house visiting your little sister Aimee. If you had not been so generous, I might never, never, never had the inclination to sit down and write my own book. In some ways, this journey all began with you.

THE DEVIL IN MIDWINTER

1.

The old folktales from Mexico often have the same beginning. "One day a man met the devil on the road," or "The devil came upon a man in the desert." This is not an old story, but I am here to tell you, I met the devil in an orchard in December. He offered me gold; he gave me pleasure; he fooled me twice and then he set me on fire.

2.

The first time I saw the devil, I took his photograph for my job at the local newspaper, *The Mattawa Weekly News*. My boss, Annie Mortmain runs the *Weekly* out of a converted goat shed on her farm. It's strictly small time—a tiny paper for a tiny town. Most of the headlines are things like "Fire Chief Retires," or "Congratulations High School Graduates." Annie owns and operates; I do the web page and Spanish translations; we both share content.

The picture with the devil in it was for a headline that would read, "New Winery to Open in Mattawa." While Annie interviewed the thrillingly handsome proprietor, Justin Colter, I tried to get his windblown blond hair, snakeskin boots and broad shoulders into focus. I failed miserably. His broad grin and blue eyes made my hands clammy and the camera kept slipping.

Annie wasn't faring a whole lot better. She conducted the interview on the site of his new tasting room and she kept stammering into her notebook, squinting through the brisk wind while her gold glasses slipped down her nose. I think we were both drooling a little. In a town where most of the eligible men are aging farmers in polyester slacks or young Mexican kids with no job prospects, Justin Colter looked like a juicy pine tree in a forest of bristly oxtongue. He smelled like sagebrush and Bay Rum. His button down shirt displayed a tantalizing tuft of gold hair; his sleeves were rolled up to show off nicely molded forearms. Even in the midwinter chill, with a wind blowing off the river, he seemed confident and comfortable in his shirtsleeves, boots planted on uneasy earth like he'd already put down roots.

"So what made you pick the town of Mattawa for your new vineyard, um, Mr. Colter?" Annie asked.

"Call me Justin," he said, with such a disarming smile that Annie, usually imperturbable, giggled. I managed to snap a picture before the camera slipped again.

"Justin, then." A blush crept over Annie's freckles. "Um, why our little town?"

"Well, Annie—" Annie blushed even more furiously at her name on his firm and shapely lips "—eastern Washington grapes and wines are making a name for themselves all over the world. I want to get in on the action here. I have a feeling it's a very special place."

I looked through the camera's viewfinder, fiddling with the focus. Behind Colter, a phalanx of construction workers busied themselves, framing a building, digging postholes, mixing cement. Hammers rattled, trucks rumbled. Around the building site, grape arbors radiated on the hillside in symmetrical rust-colored stripes. I tried to snap another picture of Colter, and frowned at the digital display. His image remained blurry. I turned the camera to the hillside, to the fresh wood on the new building, to a sign that said, "Future Site of Calyx Vineyards." All those pictures were fine. Back to Colter, focus problems again. I cursed under my breath.

By then Annie was winding up the interview. "Well, we sure are glad to welcome you to the neighborhood, Justin," she was saying with real enthusiasm.

"My pleasure, Annie. And um…" he gestured at me.

"This is my assistant, Esmeralda Ulloa," said Annie.

"Call me Esme," I said, still distracted by the camera.

"You're far too beautiful to be behind that lens," said Colter. My heart jumped as he reached out and took the camera from my damp hands. "A woman like you should be in front of a camera, always."

I saw a shadow move on the hillside as he snapped a picture. He said softly, "Just look at me, Esme," and I did, as he snapped again. He squinted at the digital display and nodded to himself. "Gotcha," he said. He looked up. "Have you ever modeled professionally?"

I couldn't answer. My mouth was as dry as a wad of paper. I didn't know if I was angry or flustered or what. It was Annie who said, "Esme's getting her English degree at the college while she works part time for me."

"English?"

"I like stories," I said, finally finding my voice.

"I like them too," Colter twinkled. "Almost as much as I like making wine."

"Esme's uncle manages Olstein Orchards," Annie said. "Not far from here."

I watched Colter's blond eyebrows quirk and his mouth lift in another knee melting smile. "Ashmead Kernal," he said. "Golden Russet, right? Famous heirloom apples? That Olstein Orchards?"

"My uncle's specialty," I said proudly.

"Then I want to meet him. The Kernals make a very nice cider."

"Yes, they do," I said. "We live right over the hill there," I added, pointing.

His gaze didn't follow my finger. He was looking down at the camera's digital display. "If I put this face on every one of my bottles, I'm pretty sure I'd make a mint." His blue eyes swept mine. "Let me know if I can. I'll write up a contract. Tiger Eye Chardonnay sounds good." He seemed to be trying the name out on his tongue, but I got the feeling a part of him was tasting my image as well. "Maybe Goddess Pinot Gris." He laughed quietly and then handed the camera back to me. It was warm from his touch and I almost dropped it.

"We should head back," said Annie, looking from him to me, her eyes narrowed behind her glinting glasses.

"I'd like a print of that picture," said Colter. His lips lifted again and I felt my pulse hammer a notch faster. "And tell me when I can come see those apples."

❄

"Good Lord," said Annie, when we were in her truck and back on the highway a few minutes later. The truck's heat was on high, cherry trees fanned out on either side of us, and Annie's gray-gold hair blew around her face in the heater's blast. "I have never seen a handsomer man. He practically radiated sex appeal. And he was certainly flirting with you."

"I couldn't even take his picture," I admitted. "He made me too nervous. I got a nice one of the building frame though."

Annie laughed. "Hell's bells, I barely got the interview. I tell you what, when the handsomest man in the world is talking, apparently even all an old woman like me can do is giggle like a school girl." She snorted. "I can see the article now. A nice headline, a blurry photo and copy that says, 'Whoo-hoo, there's a MAN in town!'" She slid me a look. "What did you think of him?"

"He came on a little strong," I said.

"I'd like to come see your apples sometime," Annie intoned in a gruff voice. We both laughed.

I glanced down at the camera in my lap. "Do you think he was serious about putting me on his wine labels? Or was he handing me a line?"

"He was doing something, sweetie, but I don't know what."

"Wow."

"Wow is right." Annie clucked her tongue as she maneuvered the wheel. "Said he picked this place to move to after growing grapes in

Italy. Can you beat that?"

"From Italy to Washington?"

Annie shrugged. "It's beautiful here. And he says the Mattawa wines will be better than the Italian ones some day. 'My wines will defy the world,' and I quote." She smiled, as she pulled into the dirt road that led to her farmhouse.

"Really." I let that idea settle in my tingling midsection.

"Did he take a nice picture of you?" Annie asked, parking by the old goat shed that housed *The Mattawa Weekly* offices.

"I guess." I flipped her the camera. She looked at the display and whistled.

"Boy," she said. "That's something." He had caught me with my lips parted, a breeze blowing back my dark brown hair. Green eyes wide, their expression fierce with a mixture of outrage and pleasure. "Tiger eyes indeed." She turned to me with a wink. "The camera's supposed to capture your soul, Esme. What does this picture say about yours?"

"That I'm longing to rip off Justin Colter's clothes, I guess."

Annie snorted, "Get in line, girl. Get in line."

Annie lives by herself on twenty acres of scrub, right next to an apple orchard. She runs the paper, breeds Pyrenean Mountain Dogs in a giant kennel up the hill, smokes a corncob pipe on her back porch and doesn't answer to anyone. She hired me two years ago as an intern, to help her put the newspaper's archives online. Since then, she's started paying me and trained me to do everything else. She swears when I graduate from college next year, she'll sell the paper to me. "You could do worse with an English degree," she says.

I didn't really know if I wanted to buy, though. It's a big wide world, after all, and Mattawa, Washington, perched on the edge of it, is somewhere in between Nowhere and Nothing At All. I hungered for more. Call it the stuff of storybooks, but I dreamed of adventures, epic battles, finding my true love. I had vivid dreams of dancing in the stars with a wild-eyed man who had fiery fingertips. Somehow, I couldn't imagine anything very epic or exciting happening in my little town of apple orchards, manufactured homes, wind and sky.

Colter had caught my hunger on camera. He had looked at me, and snapped a frame with all those unspoken dreams swimming in my eyes. I kept thinking about the way he looked at me with that half smile. Like he knew all about my cravings and knew how to make them go away. I thought about him all afternoon, while I put the finishing touches on my weekly column, "News From Appletown."

"Apple Tree Man?" Annie asked, with a lifted eyebrow, when she proofed my work awhile later.

"I thought I'd do a series on 'Winter Legends,' this month," I said. "Next week, Santa Claus; then, the Midwinter Fire Festival. I'll finish it off with the El Dia de los Santos Inocentes—people always like that one."

Annie wrinkled her brow, looking at the page I'd printed. "I think I did something like that a long while back. I can't remember which holiday legends I covered, though. It sure wasn't Apple Tree Man." She read aloud, "'Wise farmers present the last apple of the season to him as a gift, by burying it in the roots of their apple trees.'" She twinkled in my direction. "Really, Esme?"

"Why not?" I said. "Sometimes Apple Tree Man gives you treasure in return."

Annie pushed the proofed pages to me. "Go over that Colter article for me again, would you? The man got me so mesmerized, I'm afraid I might have inadvertently written, 'Kiss me now,' in the copy without realizing it."

"I know what you mean," I said, pulling out a straight edge so I could read Annie's article line by line.

In the final layout, the article about Colter sat just underneath my photo, above the fold. Annie had chosen the picture of the Calyx Vineyards sign, with the half built tasting room in the background. A black haired workman stood next to the sign, his face turned away, a wheelbarrow poised near his strong thighs, his hand cupping a match against the wind. I could see why she chose it. It was a vibrant, strong picture, full of lines and shadows, eye-catching next to the headline. I peered at the workman, trying to make out his features while something vibrated, first in my head, then in my heart.

"Esme?" Annie said. "Is there something wrong?"

I turned to her. "I know this guy," I said, pointing to the photo.

"Oh? Who is he?" Annie squinted.

I stood there, finger on the page, shaking my head, feeling a sudden tidal wave of feeling rise in my chest, threatening to choke me. *His cheekbones like blades, the shadow of his eyelashes stark in the strong sunlight.*

"Who is he?" Annie repeated.

I groped for the words. "I think I've seen him in my dreams," I said, finally. And then I burst into horrified tears.

3.

"There, there," Annie murmured a little while later, shoving a cup of tea into my shaking hands and patting my shoulder.

She had hustled my hide out of the goat shed and into her house, where she quickly put on the kettle and flipped the switch for a propane fire. Three of her huge, white dogs sniffed me with concern. Tears still rolled down my cheeks and I took in great gulps of air, like a fish yanked from the river. One of the dogs waved its plumed tail in my face. "What is happening to me?" I gasped through a mouthful of fur.

"If I had to guess, I'd say repressed memory, but I'm no expert." Annie's voice was calm. "Fluff, Blob and Fitzsimmons," she added to the dogs. "Sit, you ridiculous animals." They ignored her and started licking my knees, making my jeans damp.

"Repressed what?" I asked, absently patting Fitz. All the dogs were covered with masses of silky white fur and looked exactly like friendly polar bears. Their presence calmed me considerably, which was probably why Annie had let them in the house in the first place.

"Sometimes the mind blocks a traumatic memory," Annie

explained. "You 'forget' something that happened, so you don't have to feel the pain of it. Then the memories resurface as dreams. Or a song, a smell, a word can suddenly trigger them. Judging from what's going on with you, I'd say that photo triggered something just now."

"You're saying my dreams might be real?"

"Are they traumatic?"

I shook my head. "They're always wonderful," I said as Blob and Fluff vied with Fitzsimmons for my attention, thrusting their square heads under my palms. "I usually wake up sad, though." I shook my head. "It's like… I know him? The boy in the picture. I know him better than anyone? But I don't know who he is."

Annie said quietly, "You said 'boy.' That there's a picture of a young man."

I turned to her. "What do you think that means?"

"That he is—or looks very much like someone you knew long ago," Annie said. "Someone you tried to forget, maybe."

"But who? And why?"

"I'm sure it'll come to you sooner or later."

I buried my hands in Fluff's white fur. "Annie. What could I have repressed?"

She looked carefully at me through her gold glasses. "Lots of things, Esme. Your life is not without its traumas. You and your brothers are orphans. Your uncle found you in Arizona somewhere and took you in, but you've never said a thing about what your life was like before he found you."

"I don't remember," I said promptly and then clapped my hand over my mouth.

"Exactly," Annie nodded. "I suspect there's a lot you don't know about yourself. A lot you 'don't remember' from your early life. Maybe it's time to remember, now."

"I'm not sure I want to," I said as Fluff licked my nose.

Annie said simply. "Drink your tea, Esmeralda. And then I think you'd better go home and ask your Uncle Oscar some questions about this man in the picture. Who he is, or who he might look like."

"Have you ever had a dream come to life, Annie?"

Annie leaned across the waving dog tails and patted my damp knee. She said, "I can't say I have, but maybe you're luckier than most, Esmeralda."

"I don't feel lucky," I said.

"Tell me what you remember about your dreams."

I leaned back. "They always start the same way," I said slowly. "I... I dance in heaven with a gray-eyed boy. It's cold in the stars, but he keeps me warm by holding me close." Feeling a little embarrassed to be saying it out loud, I glanced at Annie. But she just looked kindly back and nodded encouragingly. I said, "Sometimes we fly together in a dark blue sky, with silver fire raining around. Sometimes he tells me stories, wonderful ones that I never remember. Sometimes, we have long conversations and he tries to teach me things. Sometimes his face changes, and instead of gray eyes and black hair, he looks another way. But I know him; I know him as well as I know my way home through the orchards. I know him even though I don't remember his name." I shook my head. "And saying all of this out loud just makes it seem like a load of crap, by the way."

Annie just said, "It sounds like your mind is trying to tell you something, but I'm damned if I know what."

❄

I drove home later that evening through gathering gloom, down secret dirt roads to my uncle's orchards. Fear pricked my arms, slid around in my belly, trembled on my mouth. A print of the Calyx vineyard picture lay on the front seat beside me. I kept reaching out to touch the face of the young man. Seeing him made me ache all over. Who was he to me? And why couldn't I remember him?

I was so wrapped up, I almost ran over the man staggering through the trees. He burst out of a grove right in front of me and collapsed on the gravel. Immediately, I slammed on the brakes, jerking the wheel to the side, narrowly missing a tree. I scrabbled with the seatbelt, throwing open the door to see if he was all right.

He lay prone in the middle of the road, his hands over his head, as if protecting it from assault. "Sir?" I said. "Señor? Are you all right—" I reached for his shoulder and he shrieked, scrabbling away from me on all fours, eyes wide in his face. He had the dark, seamed skin of a lifelong farm worker. His palms, torn from skidding on gravel, were sticky with blood.

I spoke softly in Spanish. "Please, sir. I'm just here to help you. Look at me. I am Esmeralda, of the orchard of Mr. Olstein. Can I call someone for you? Do you need an ambulance? Did someone hurt you? Do I call the police?"

He said hoarsely in Spanish, "There is a devil in the trees. I saw him on his horse, and he tried to eat me." He put his face in his bleeding hands and sobbed like a child.

Moving slowly, so as not to alarm him, I took my cell phone out of my pocket and called emergency services. Then I sat on the chilly gravel, the headlights of my car shining, and held him, while cold and darkness oozed around us. He babbled and wept, telling a long, rambling story about needing to contact a bruja, or witch, who lived across the river. "She must come to give us protection, but she doesn't like to cross the water," he said, over and over. I patted his back and murmured soothing nonsense to calm him.

At last a pair of paramedics from the Fire Department came crunching down the gravel in a red truck, flashing their lights. By then the man, who called himself Paco Fernandez, had quieted somewhat. He refused to go at first, because he feared leaving me alone in the orchard. He insisted I would be attacked by the devil and his horse as well, if left on my own. I assured him I was getting in my car and driving straight to my uncle's house. Paco scrabbled at his throat for a crucifix, and tried to give it to me. I refused, pressing the chain back into his bloody hands. He started to weep again as a medic led him away.

"Where will you take him?" I asked.

"To Urgent Care. It's got to be drugs." The other paramedic shook his head. "There's some kind of really bad stuff going around, because we keep getting these calls. Devils in the trees, monsters walking among us, crap like that. Happy holidays, right?"

The journalist in me pricked up her ears. "A lot of calls?" It sounded like something I should mention to Annie.

The paramedic shrugged and nodded, heading for the truck. The whole thing probably bored him. Small towns and rural areas are always full of drugs. It comes with the territory, along with poverty and violence.

I waved encouragingly to Paco. Then I stood in the road, watching the ambulance disappear, siren silent. Blinking red lights threw flickering flame-like highlights on the tree trunks. I shivered, thinking of the devil hiding in the shadows.

I got into my car, making a mental note to follow up at the clinic, and maybe with the police and fire services tomorrow, as well. If there were multiple calls about monsters in the trees, *The Mattawa Weekly* ought to do a story.

In the front seat of my car, the picture from the paper stared up at me. The young worker, so familiar and so strange at the same time, still cupped his hands around a flame. I touched his face. "Who are you and what is happening to me?" I whispered. I put the car in gear, hoping my uncle would have some answers.

But by the time I got home that night, Uncle Oscar had already gone out for the evening, and so I couldn't ask him about the man in the photograph. My younger brothers were deep into a loud game of Call of Duty on the video screen. I knew better than to interrupt them with a question about some stranger in a picture. After standing in the kitchen for a while, not sure what to do, I gave up and slammed into my room. There I huddled on the bed, fully expecting to be up half the night waiting for my uncle to get home so I could question him. Instead, I fell asleep almost immediately, while my brothers cheered and screamed in the living room, the mechanized sounds of war on full volume, seeming to vibrate the walls of our house.

4.

THE DEVIL AND HIS GARDEN
A fairy story

The Devil walked on a road in the desert, and he was very angry. All around him the birds built nests and the plants blossomed in flowers and the bees made honey. But the Devil could make nothing at all because the Devil is not a maker; the Devil only corrupts.

He looked at the ants, so busy expanding their cities, the moles, so diligently digging their holes. Even the wasps industriously transformed plant stems into paper. The Devil came to a decision. "I must make something, too," he thought. "I will grow a garden, and make fruits and flowers for my own delight."

So the Devil watched the farmers plant and nurture the soil. And he bargained with them for seeds; he pestered them for a plot of land; he cajoled them to teach him how to grow. He cultivated the soil and planted the seeds just as he had been instructed. But nothing grew in the Devil's soil, nothing at all, just ashes and smoke, cinders and slag. For the Devil is not a grower of fruits. The Devil is only a gambler.

5.

The dream started the way it always did; we danced in the blue heavens, with stars all around. He held me in his arms. I could feel the silky skirt I wore floating around my thighs as we turned and turned. I knew everything about him. He had a little constellation of freckles on his neck in the shape of a cross; flecks of gold lightning decorated his storm gray eyes; he had a habit of tossing his head to get the long black hair out of his face. He was going to kiss me tonight, I was absolutely sure of it. I watched his lips curl in a smile. He knew what I was thinking.

"It's lessons tonight, chica, not kisses," he said.

"I'd rather kisses," I said.

He leaned in close. "You have a test tomorrow, cara."

His hair brushed my cheek. It tickled. "So let's review the answers. Who am I?"

That was easy. "You are my true love."

"Who are you?"

"I am the sleeping princess," I said, although I felt wide-awake and happier than I ever had been.

"What kind of story is this?"

I looked at the freckles on his neck and leaned forward to press my mouth on them. His skin burned under my lips. I could feel his heart beat in my mouth. "Please, no lessons tonight," I implored. "You're leaving me."

He stopped moving and the stars all around resolved themselves into twinkling shapes. He put his fingers, hot as firecrackers, in my hair and stroked. "I'm coming back, Esme. It's time to wake up, my love."

"I don't want to wake up from this," I breathed. "Please."

He plucked a star from the sky and gave it to me. It twinkled in my palm. "What do you make of that?" he said.

I closed my fist and looked in his eyes. I opened my hand, and a bright red flower lay on my palm, soft as a whisper. "There," I said. "Now will you kiss me?"

His warm mouth came down on mine and immediately it began to rain stars all around us. I laughed even as I kissed him and I felt his answering laugh on my tongue as light drizzled and dropped, dissolving and resolving into a magical glass house, like a fairy palace, with rain rattling on the roof in a wild thrum. It was daylight, and now Uncle Oscar had taken my hand and said, "Push your fingers right in the dirt, Esmeralda."

I could clearly see the black hairs on his strong arms as he placed my small palm in cool, dark brown earth, the same color as Oreo cookies. The dirt smelled loamy and good. I felt a soft, wonderful tingling and trembling in my skin. "It tickles," I told Uncle Oscar.

"Good!" he said. "That's very good. Keep digging, preciosa. Dig with your hands."

I dug, letting my hands be earthmovers, letting them be small burrowing animals, letting them be worms in the ground. After awhile though, I got very sleepy and my head felt heavy, so I put it right down on the dirt where my hands were buried and I dreamed my mind drained right out of my ear and into the ground itself. My mind had eyes of its own and they saw how gold leaked out of my fingers and filled the earth with a kind of radiant light.

"It is bad for you to use her this way," said a voice from above me,

somewhere in the glass walls of the fairy house. It was a husky voice, tinged with bitterness, like a cup of very strong tea. "Her gifts aren't something you just take, Oscar, you have to give something back."

"She will want for nothing. And I will have everything." Uncle Oscar's warm, confident voice wove in and out of the glass panes of the crystal house, like a gold bee flying in and out of a window on a beam of sunlight. Rain poured; I slept and inside the tub of earth the light drained out of my hands and colored each Oreo grain with gleaming gold.

❄

"Xavier," I whispered, as I woke from my dream.

"What?" my brother Ignacio said from my bedroom door. He was munching an apple, a grin on his face. It was morning and I had slept in my clothes.

I groaned, flopping on my pillow, shaking the dream out of my head. "What are you doing in here?" I demanded.

He shrugged. Both my brothers are handsome, both still in high school. They play soccer, make piles of dirty laundry, stomp around in big boots and drive me nuts. I love them. "You left your phone in the kitchen," Ignacio said. "Damned thing won't stop buzzing. Someone really wants to get a hold of you." He crossed the room and placed the phone in my slack hand. "You don't get undressed for bed anymore?"

"Oh, hush," I waved him away as I checked my telephone for messages. "Don't you have to go to school or something?"

Annie had called and texted me multiple times. Most of the messages said the same thing. Justin Colter had been calling the newspaper, over and over again, asking for me, asking for a copy of my picture. Annie's last message said something like, "Call the damn man before I drive over and kill him. Some of us have work to do today." I laughed and called Colter right away, my heart speeding like a hummingbird's.

"I've been learning all about your uncle's heirloom apples," came Colter's rich voice over the line. The image of his tanned forearms and blue eyes danced into my brain.

"They're Olstein's Orchards," I said. "Uncle Oscar just manages them."

"Which means your uncle is the one who makes the fruit what it is. Olstein just owns the land, right?"

"Yes, that's exactly right."

"I know how this works, Esmeralda. Your uncle is the talent. Websites all over the world are raving about his fruit." His voice changed a little, dropping in volume as he said suddenly, "What are you doing right now?"

I had, in fact, been using my free hand to unbutton my blouse, changing out of the wrinkled clothes I had slept in. I wanted to get a jump on my day, but now I felt self-conscious, like Colter could see what I was doing. I clutched my collar quickly and said, "Getting ready for school. It's finals week and I have an exam today."

"Oh? In what?" His voice was still conspiratorial, like he knew perfectly well I had been undressing while I talked to him. I felt my face grow hot.

"Folklore and Mythology of the Americas," I said, sounding angrier than I felt.

Colter chuckled, as if he found something funny. "Did you cover the Mexican myths?"

"Of course."

"You have a favorite? Quetzacoatl? His brother Xoloti?"

"'The Story of the Fifth Sun' is my favorite, I think, but I like them all," I said. "What's a winemaker doing reading Mexican myths?"

Colter laughed lightly. "I can't write stories, so I guess I like to read them. What about you?"

"Sometimes I think there's more truth to a story than to real life. Is that weird?"

"Not weird, Esme." Colter said my name gently, like he'd just kissed me with it. "Stories tell all sorts of truths. But the truths are twisted with a thousand beautiful lies. And how do you tell the difference?"

"It's something I feel," I whispered.

His voice brimmed with laughter. "What are you feeling right now?"

I felt desire, pure and simple. It was as if Colter had reached through the telephone and started stroking me. My skin tingled. My lips buzzed. My heart beat a tattoo on my ribs. My thighs parted, aching for his hand to slip between them. "I… don't know," I stammered.

"Is that right?" He chuckled. "Well. When do you get done with your test?"

"Um, why?"

"I want to see you. I want a copy of that picture I took of you yesterday. I want to meet your uncle."

"You want a lot." I tried to insert a light note into my thickening voice.

"I might have a proposition."

"For my uncle or for me?"

"Make an appointment, let's find out."

I wanted to take my clothes off and jump into his arms. I wanted to run away as fast as a deer. And I wanted to cry my heart out for what I didn't have.

"I have to go," I said out loud.

"Can I see you this afternoon?" The eagerness in his voice gave me a thrill, even as it scared me.

I said, "I'll be back from my exam at two. I'll meet you at the entrance to Olstein's on Road T. You know where that is?"

"I know where to find you," Colter said quietly. "I'm looking forward to it, Esme."

I hung up and gazed at my reflection in the mirror. I looked positively wanton, my blouse unbuttoned, my long hair a tangled mess from sleeping. I thought of Colter's broad chest, his gold hair, his grin. Then I practically ran into the shower, purposefully making the water as cold as I could stand.

After showering, I texted my uncle about Colter. With the harvest over, his schedule was flexible and a meeting was surely possible at two. "And then I can ask him about the man in the photo," I thought, as I dashed out to my car, a thermos of coffee in my hand, the Calyx Vineyards picture folded in my pocket, a knapsack slung over my shoulder.

Driving out of the orchard to the highway, I kept thinking I caught glimpses of someone walking in the groves beside me. I focused my eyes on the road while my car bounced and jiggled, but a tall man, all dressed in black, crossed my peripheral vision again and again. Sometimes he was just ahead, sometimes he was just behind, but impossibly he kept pace with the car. I remembered Paco the night before, and his raving about demons in the trees. I felt little ripples of fear run up and down my spine. I knew it was silly, but in the end, I was very glad to be turning onto the highway, heading towards school, out of the groves, into the busy, mundane world of stoplights, parking lots, classes, exams. And that was all I thought about until Annie called me about the murder.

6.

My head was still filled with my final exam when I felt my phone buzz in the student union some hours later. "Quetzalcoatl gave corn to mankind just as Changing Woman taught the Navajo how to live…" "There were five suns in Aztec mythology, four worlds in the creation stories of the early North Americans…" and then there was Annie's voice over the phone saying, "They think it's a murder," and I said, "I'm sorry. What?"

The connection, full of static, distorted Annie's voice but even so I could hear worry and exasperation. "The family only speaks Spanish; I can't get a statement from them. I wondered if you could follow up for me. If you don't have time today, I get it. We just put last week's issue to bed. But if you had a chance this weekend…"

"Wow, Annie." Murders were not frequent in our little town, but sometimes they happened, mostly with the young, out-of-work boys. "Is this gang related?"

"No, that's the really weird part. He's an older man, a farmer. They found his body face down in an irrigation ditch. That's odd in and of itself, but I guess he'd also been burned severely."

"What?" my voice barked. The connection was very bad indeed. Had I heard right?

"Unofficially, the police think he caught on fire, and then tried to put it out by breaking through the ice in the irrigation ditch. But they're not sure if he died from burns, or from drowning, or something else. They're not even sure how he caught on fire in the first place and they won't know until they check for accelerants. Maybe it was drugs or drink. Maybe murder." Annie's usually hearty voice sounded husky, even through the pop and crack of the weak connection.

"That's gruesome." I shuddered, imagining flames, panic, then icy mud, dark, cold water. I fiddled with a pen and a scrap of paper. "What's the family name, Annie?"

"Fernandez. They're on Ellice Street."

"Oh." My throat closed and my lips went suddenly numb.

"Are you all right, Esme?" Annie asked, hearing the change in my voice. "Was he somebody you knew?"

I thought of the man from last night, the one I had sent away with the paramedics. His name had been Paco Fernandez, and he was older, a farmer. The town Urgent Care Clinic, where the paramedics had taken him, sat right near a large irrigation ditch. "I don't know," I said, clearing my throat. "Maybe. There are a lot of Fernandez families in town, though."

"Esme? You don't have to do this. Follow up, I mean. I realize you have a couple of days off, probably holiday shopping to do, your exam..."

"My exam's over. I'll try to get this done, Annie," I said. I hung up the phone with shaking hands.

❄

The college is a fifty-minute drive from Mattawa. My uncle had left a message that he would be delighted to meet with Colter at two. The exam had taken two full hours, which meant I barely had enough time to drive back home before meeting Colter at the entrance to Olstein Orchards. I felt sick and dizzy, not up to the long drive. I found a bench in the student union and sat down, putting my head between my knees until the world stopped tilting.

When my head cleared, I tried calling Colter on my cell phone to cancel the appointment. I wanted to know, with an urgency I couldn't explain, if the murdered Paco Fernandez was the same person I had met in the orchards the night before. But it was lunchtime, and the student union filled, as hundreds of chattering people lined up at a nearby food court. My phone wouldn't work. I stepped outside to see if I could find quiet and a better connection. I was checking the phone display for bars when I banged right into someone's chest.

I glanced up, an apology already forming on my lips, but shock wiped my mind clean. Because he stood there, the man from my dreams, the man in the photograph. It was as if he had sprung from the ground, dressed in black from the tips of his boots to the collar of his jacket. His hair glimmered like a raven's wing. His eyes were the color of a summer thunderstorm.

The dizziness I'd felt a moment before overwhelmed me. My knees crumpled, dark spots bloomed in front of my eyes. I swayed, and the next thing I knew, I was in his arms, pressed up against the brick wall of the student union building, his lips a centimeter from my own.

Heat from his body radiated, tangible and delicious, like glowing coals. I registered rock hard arms, his thighs pressed against mine. His skin smelled of cedar fires, fragrant, musky and sweet all at once. My chest tightened. "Esmeralda," he murmured. His voice was deep and it vibrated through my core.

I managed to whisper, "How are you here?" I looked around me, at the endless stream of students filing in and out of the glass doors of the building, at the parking lot over his shoulder. "You—You go to school at Washington Central?" I asked inanely.

He shook his head. "No. It's just easier to talk to you in this place.

Back home—it's still hard to get through."

"Then—I'm not—hallucinating?" My heart hammered in my ears and I thought I might faint.

"Oh, chica." I felt the muscles in his arms bunch as he held me tighter. "No. I'm here."

He felt solid enough, his warms arms embracing me. "Where do you come from? How—"

He shook his head, cutting me off. "There's no time. You have to go soon. You have to meet with Colter as soon as you can."

"I wanted to go to Ellice Street—"

"That can wait," he said firmly. "Remember the test?"

"I just took a test," I said, random bits of Central American folklore flicking through my brain. *Nanahuatzin jumped into the fire and became the sun…*

"No, the real test. Do you remember?" His gray eyes searched my face.

"Remember what?"

His hands slid down my arms, their heat tracing a wonderful fire from my shoulders to my wrists. He gripped my fingers. "Who are you?"

"I am the sleeping princess," I said automatically.

He closed his eyes, long black lashes sweeping his cheekbones. "Yes. And they will bargain for you like a lamb on the block. But you are old enough to choose. If you ask, it will be given. Do you understand?"

"No—"

He opened his eyes. I saw sunbeams on storm clouds. "You have to wake up," he said. And then before I could say another word he kissed me fiercely.

The touch of his mouth rocketed through me. Fire raced down my spine as I opened my lips, tasting him, sweet and fierce. I felt a flash in my chest, like lightning in an empty sky. I pressed my body into his, as an exquisite whirlpool of pleasure began to swirl in my center.

My phone buzzed in my hands, startling us both. He pulled away, breathing heavily. "The bastard has fingers even here," he said, voice husky.

"I don't have to answer this."

"You do," he said shakily. His lips crooked in a smile. "There's no time. Esme." His hot hand touched my cheek briefly. "Remember me, love."

I wanted him to kiss me again. He didn't, though. Instead, I watched as he put his hands together; I saw a fire kindle in his palms. He blew it fiercely in my direction. I felt the warmth blast on my face. Then the phone buzzed again and he disappeared as suddenly as he had manifested.

My phone clattered unanswered on the sidewalk as I leaned up against the wall pressing my palms into the bricks until they hurt, my rapid breath making little white puffs in the air. I don't know how long I stood, feeling hot and cold, frightened and safe, while students poured in and out of the doors nearby. I wondered if I had dreamed the whole thing. I wondered if I was losing my mind. I thought about what Annie had said about repressed memory and clenched my teeth until my jaw hurt. I wanted to remember him. I wanted to remember everything about him with a craving so deep, my whole body ached, as if remembering were a balm for an illness that went all the way to the marrow of my bones.

Eventually, I shakily retrieved my phone from the freezing sidewalk and listened to the message. It was Colter, wondering if he could meet me a little earlier than we'd planned. I scanned the cold campus for my dream man, but saw only strangers. I wondered again if he was real, if I was mad. Then I called Colter back and told him I was on my way.

7.

THE STORY OF THE VOLCANO
An Aztec Myth

Once upon a time there was a princess named Iztaccihuatl, more beautiful than any woman, and a handsome warrior Popocatepetl, who loved her. They were to be married, and all the kingdoms rejoiced. But war broke out on the eve of their wedding, so Popocatepetl had to kiss his intended and tell her he must fight. He promised to return victorious from battle and make her his wife.

But while Popocatepetl fought bravely, the Devil slipped into Iztaccihuatl's house and said her beloved had died in the war and would not be returning. Overwhelmed by sadness, the beautiful princess slipped into a sleep like death and would not awaken.

When Popocatepetl returned victorious, he received the terrible news of his beloved's death. Try as he might, he could not awaken her. He wandered the streets like a ghost, tearing at his clothes.

One day Popocatepetl ordered a great tomb be built under the sun. He piled ten hills together to make a huge mountain. He carried the sleeping princess in his arms all the way to the top. There he kissed her lips, took up a smoking torch, and knelt by her side to watch over her until she would awaken and be his bride.

There they still stand, two mountains, El Popo and the White Woman; El Popo still smokes, as his vigil has never ended.

As for the Devil, he too became a mountain, Pico de Orizaba, and he watches the lovers from afar, his heart black with jealousy. For the Devil does not love, he only lusts like a dragon. Meanwhile, the lovers lie peaceful under snow, as beautiful as a dream.

8.

He waited at the gate to the orchards, slouched behind the wheel of a gigantic black Ford pickup truck. I pulled up beside him and rolled down my passenger side window. "Follow me," I yelled.

"Gladly," he said, with one of his slow smiles. "Did you remember your Mexican gods?"

"Of course. I remember everything," I said.

"Do you?"

I nodded, put the car in gear and gripped the wheel very tightly. Between Colter, the dark man, and Paco Fernandez I felt like my life was a drawer full of random junk that had been upended. I wanted to sift through everything, think about it, sort it, but there wasn't time. I checked the rearview mirror to make sure Colter was behind me. His huge truck loomed, the great chrome grate seeming to smile coldly at my little car. I had the sensation we were moving very quickly, although we both inched down the dirt roads at a sedate speed.

Uncle Oscar waited for us in the apple grove he called his "laboratory." Although he husbanded thousands of trees that bore the popular supermarket apples—Golden Delicious, Honeycrisp, Fuji, my uncle specialized in reviving antique and heritage varieties, ones with funny names like "Caville Blanc," "Ashmead Kernal," and "Pitmason Pineapple." Most of the heirloom apples he grew did not look like much—they were small, misshapen, sometimes speckled like eggs. In the supermarket, they'd be passed right over for bigger, prettier varieties. But my uncle's apples tasted like poems in the mouth, and all over the world gourmet chefs, makers of specialty ciders, or just people who appreciated flavor and novelty in their food knew about his orchard laboratory, and his strange, spotted fruit.

I watched my uncle take the measure of Colter as he swung down from his truck and shook his hand. Brown eyes looked up into blue. I saw something flicker on my uncle's face, a kind of uneasiness I had never seen before. Colter said, "I think you've got some things I want, Mr. Ulloa."

My uncle withdrew his hand and held it to his chest, almost like it had been stung. He hesitated and looked at me. Then he said to Colter, "Why don't you come into my office and we can talk?"

I started to follow them into the corrugated tin shed that served double duty as storage, workshop and office for my uncle, but he hesitated. ",," he said, suddenly speaking Spanish. He still held his hand close to his body. "I-I would like it very much if you found Mr. Colter here some, uh, some samples of the apples, so he could taste them. Would you mind doing that?"

I answered in English, to be polite, in case Colter didn't understand us. "No. I don't mind getting him some apples." I shot Colter a look.

He smiled, his head cocked to one side, and said very clearly in Spanish, "Please. I'd enjoy tasting your apples very much."

My uncle shook his head, bit his lip and tossed me a set of keys. I snatched them from the air, wondering what I had missed between them. They ambled into the shed. My uncle's shoulders tightened. Colter threw me a wink. Then the door closed behind them.

"They will bargain for you like a lamb on the block," my dream man's words came back to me. But that made no sense, I thought to myself. How could they bargain for me? I was almost twenty-one, with my whole life ahead of me. I clenched the keys in my hand and walked away.

Uncle Oscar stored sample heirloom apples in another shed next to his office, in bins and a large walk in refrigerator. I let myself in the door and quickly filled a burlap sack with an assortment of his best: the beautiful Arkansas Blacks, juicy Ashmead Kernals, Burford Reds with their pretty crimson skin.

During harvest time, my little brothers swear that the smell of apples sickens them, the way it washes up from the bags we wear while picking, how it almost steams in big wafts from the wooden harvest boxes. But I could fill my house with tart-sugary scent and never get tired of it. In the winter, the smell of apples is like a little message from summer, a promise of warm days and sweetness to come.

When I returned to my uncle's office, and let myself inside, the tension between he and Colter appeared to have dissipated. They were laughing like old friends and had uncorked one of Uncle Oscar's homemade hard cider bottles. They held aloft half-filled jam jars, as if in mid-toast. On the table between them lay one of my uncle's little, hand-carved boxes.

When he wasn't growing fruit, Uncle Oscar carved many such chests, palm-sized, often with pretty designs festooning the lids. They littered his office, stacked on the shelves, scattered throughout the jumble of papers, files, order forms and equipment. He gave them away as gifts, and sometimes sold them at the local farmers' markets. This box looked particularly old, its elaborate carvings worn and dark.

I delivered the bag of heirlooms into Colter's outstretched hand. He glanced at me, blue eyes appraising. Uncle Oscar also looked up too, a funny little sadness on his face. His finger gently brushed some dust from the wooden box.

"Your uncle's been telling me about how he took you and your brothers in," Colter said. "It almost sounds like a fairy story, Esmeralda. Only instead of being a poor wood cutter, he's a poor farmer..."

"And instead of finding a magical princess, he found a pack of pains-in-the-neck," I said quickly with a grin at my uncle.

"That's how you tell it," Colter said. "I'm not sure your uncle would agree."

Uncle Oscar stirred in his seat and his chair creaked. "I took you kids in, and I've never regretted a single second of it, Esme." His voice was soft.

"You've been just like a father," I said. I turned to Colter. "He's even paying for my college classes."

"Well, why wouldn't he?" Colter grinned at my uncle.

"I always wanted Esmeralda to get out of this little town, afterwards. See the world. Maybe live in a big city, have her own life." Again, Uncle Oscar reached out a finger and brushed the box.

"Is that what you want, Esmeralda?" asked Colter.

I looked from my uncle to Colter. They both seemed intent on my answer. I could swear my uncle was holding his breath.

"I… don't know what I want," I said at last. At that moment, it was especially true. I felt like I barely knew my own name, let alone what I wanted out of my life. I added, "Uncle. Do you know who this is?"

I held out the picture from the paper. It was crumpled from being in my pocket. Uncle Oscar took the photo between his fingers, and smoothed it. He stared for a long time and then dropped it on his desk. He said, "No. I don't know who this is. Why?"

"I thought he looked familiar."

My uncle drained his cider and poured himself more, the bottle ringing against the lip of his jar. "He just looks like a lot of boys in this town." He cleared his throat.

My uncle was lying and I knew it. I reached to take the picture from his desk, more than a little angry, but Colter snatched it right out from under my fingers. He looked at it while my uncle drained his glass again. "Well," said Colter. "This is an interesting picture." He cocked his head. "A very bold juxtaposition, wouldn't you say, Oscar?" He looked at me. "Who did you say he is to you?"

"I'm not sure," I snapped, suddenly fed up with strange tension, my uncle's avoidance, the way every second sentence out of Colter's mouth seemed to be some kind of snide entendre. I said to Uncle Oscar, "I have some things to do for Annie this afternoon. Will you and Mr. Colter be okay if I cut out?"

My uncle just stared at the box, clutching his glass. It was Colter who answered, blue eyes narrowing. "Call me Justin, Esmeralda," he said. He leaned back in his chair, adding, "I'd like to call you later, if that's all right. I've got some wine labels I still want to talk about, and a picture of yours I'd like your permission to play with. Maybe we can make an exchange of sorts."

I looked at Uncle Oscar. He seemed to have no opinion on the matter, so finally I nodded. "That would be fine," I said. "I'll be home as soon as I can," I added to my uncle, making no effort to keep the anger from my voice. He just nodded, eyes on the little wooden box.

❄

I drove into town, feeling almost as rattled as my little car, bouncing on dirt roads. Why had my uncle lied about the boy in the picture? What had been going on between him and Colter? And what was I to make of my dream man, his cryptic pleadings, his talk of a "test"? Had the conversation happened? Was he even real? Because if there had been a "test," I hadn't taken it. I had only seen two men, sharing a riddle they wouldn't explain.

I wondered again if I was going crazy. I'd read enough books about schizophrenia to know that people who had the condition lived in imaginary worlds, talked to people who weren't there and often thought everyone around them was involved in a weird conspiracy. *Was something like that happening to me?*

I wrenched my attention to the present moment. I was supposed to be following up a story for the newspaper. Annie had said the

Fernandez family lived on Ellice Street. Setting my teeth, I turned the wheel of my car and focused my mind on Paco Fernandez and the job at hand.

I wasn't sure of the exact address, but I had the right house pegged in half a block, due to the dozens of vehicles parked around it and the steady stream of people going in and out of the front door. If someone dies in a whistle-stop like Mattawa, you can count on everyone in town showing up to pay their respects. I parked my car and went up the walk, carrying a small cache of Uncle Oscar's apples, ones that I had filched from the storage unit while fetching Colter's samples.

I greeted the person answering the door very warmly, and presented my apples. She was a teenaged girl, brown eyed and brown skinned. She told me her name was Veronica and the dead man had been her grandfather. She took the bag of apples, presumably to put with other gifts of food somewhere in the house. She thanked me when I expressed my condolences. She showed me to the living room where a generous crowd of people stood around talking softly. I joined them.

I had a great many acquaintances among the well wishers. I spent a long time conversing quietly with them, gleaning what information I could about the deceased Paco Fernandez. The details of his death were disturbing.

He was indeed the Paco I had met in the orchard the night before; I could see that from the photographs decorating the mantle and scattered on top of the old television in the corner. He had been the father of five children, had worked in the orchards as a supervisor and worked in construction during the cold season. He had been picking up some extra cash, as had many men in town, on the construction site of Calyx Vineyards when he died. He had been a beloved father and grandfather, a good friend, a fine citizen. I heard absolutely nothing about monsters, devils or demons, or, for that matter, of drug use. He appeared to be, by all accounts, a good worker, devoted to his family and community. In fact, there was nothing about Paco Fernandez that would suggest he would have wound up sitting in the gravel on an orchard road, babbling hysterically about witches and devils, last night or any night of his life.

After an hour or more of small talk and consoling murmurs, I made my way to the front door, my mind filled with questions.I thought of Paco's bloodstained hands, how he had tried to protect me with a crucifix. Who—or what—was the "devil" he had met in the orchard? Why did he think it was a danger to "us"? Had the "devil" killed him? Or had he killed himself?

I had my hand on the doorknob when a voice brought me up short. It said, "Yes, he called me late last night and I came as soon as I could."

I stopped in my tracks. It was the Strong Tea Voice from my dream that morning, the person who had been talking to Uncle Oscar in the glass house. The voice was real. Just as with the dark man earlier that day, another of my dreams had sprung to life.

9.

I turned my head, this way and that, peering through the crowd of people, trying to locate the source of the voice. At last I focused on Veronica, the teenaged girl who had let me in the house. She spoke to a small woman, with sinewy brown arms, dressed in a bright green skirt that fell to the floor in a silken swirl. The woman had black eyes, graying hair and skin the color of oiled teak.

"Hey, Veronica," I said, swallowing my nervousness. "I just wanted to tell you again how sorry I am about your granddad."

Veronica nodded and the woman with the voice from my dream peered up at me, her black eyes twinkling. I said to her, in what I hoped was a casual voice, "Hello. Do I know you?"

She smiled, showing surprisingly tiny white teeth, like a baby's, swaddled in pink gums. She said, "Esmeralda Ulloa, I would hope that you know me. But I doubt you do."

I rocked back on my heels as she leaned in close, her black eyes snapping. "Tell your uncle I have what he's looking for," she said softly. "And if he asks me nicely, I might give it to him." She smiled again. "I'd rather give it to you, though. If you ask."

I gaped. Veronica looked from her to me, brown eyes wide in her pretty face. I stammered to the old woman, "Give—me what?"

She clucked, "That's entirely the wrong question, Esmeralda. Just like you've already given the wrong answer. No one can help you, if you keep doing that, child." She turned abruptly and grabbed Veronica's arm. "M'ija show me to your poor abuelita," she said to her, gesturing towards the living room.

"Wait," I cried, grabbing her. Her arm was like a piece of apple wood, hard and slender. "Do you know about… about him?" My lips trembled just thinking about the dark young man, his mouth on mine, the urgency in his stormy eyes. "Can you—can you tell me? Is he real?"

Her thin, gray eyebrows arched. She nodded. "Yes. Of course. All of this is real. As real as anything. But I can't help you until your uncle undoes what he did, or until you find a way to undo it yourself." She seemed to take pity on me and added, "I am only here today because of this family, yes? And I come at my peril. I will cross back over the river as soon as possible, before he finds me. You must call on me there, Esmeralda, as soon as you can. Veronica will tell you where to go." She turned back to the girl. "Let us see your dear grandmother," she added in Spanish, and the two of them turned their backs, leaving me gaping in the foyer.

I stumbled out in the street and into my car in a fog of confusion. The feeling of almost remembering something buzzed around in my head like a mad wasp. She had told me "all of this is real," but how could that be true? My dream man could appear and disappear like a flame in sunlight; Paco had babbled about a devil and then died a horrible death. Did this mean the devil was real? Or that a real man could vanish into thin air?

One thing was perfectly clear: I had to get home to my uncle right away; he knew a lot more than he was telling. I would sit him down and ask about this woman; I would force from him what he knew about the man he had pretended not to recognize. I would get him to tell me what in the hell had been going on between him and Colter that afternoon.

Feeling determined, I quickly called Annie, to tell her I had spoken to the deceased man's family, and they were as mystified by Paco Fernandez's murder as everyone else in town. Then I started my car and headed for home.

❄

From the Mattawa Weekly News, Dec 7, 2012
NEWS FROM APPLE TOWN
By Esmeralda Ulloa

This week I'd like to focus on the holiday legend of Apple Tree Man. This ancient spirit is supposed to watch over every fruit forest. Wise farmers present the last apple of the season to him as a gift by burying it in the roots of the trees. When they do, Apple Tree Man makes sure the next year's harvest will be plentiful. Sometimes, as an extra bonus, he leaves a pile of gold buried in the roots of the trees as well.

I don't know how much value to attach to this old story, of course, but I do know, scientifically speaking, rotten apples and old fruit make for good compost, and good compost makes for healthy trees. Healthy trees in turn make for a good harvest, which means it's practical to bury your old apples where they can do the most good. But I think there's also treasure to be had with the gesture of giving back to your trees. Maybe not literal treasure—maybe not gold, mind you—but I think humbly thanking them, giving back a little of what they so generously and faithfully gave you, will keep you respecting the harvest. And the harvest here in Apple Town, let's face it folks, is our livelihood. Respecting it, and being thankful for it, lies at the core of our community.

I promise I won't laugh at you if you sneak out too bury a few Pink Ladies at the roots of our trees this December. Assuredly, you'll be doing your part for next year's crop. And who knows? You might find some buried treasure—be it gold or simple gifts of the spirit. Happy holidays!

10.

I came home, ready to question my uncle, only to find the house in chaos and my brothers standing in the kitchen surrounded by an unbelievable mess. It looked like they had dragged every pot and pan out of the cupboards, spilled flour on every surface and then smeared a dozen eggs on the floor.

"What in the world are you doing?" I asked them.

Ignacio said, "Uncle Oscar went ballistic."

Miguel added, "He was super drunk."

I said automatically, "Uncle Oscar doesn't get drunk." Then I remembered the way he had been gulping cider earlier and felt sick to my stomach.

My brothers exchanged frightened glances. Haltingly, they told me what had happened. According to them, Uncle Oscar had stayed in his office all afternoon, presumably with Justin Colter, although neither one of my brothers had seen him or his black truck. All they knew was that by four o'clock, my uncle had been stumbling drunk and had come roaring into the house, shouting my name at the top of his lungs. When he discovered I was not home, he proceeded to knock the kitchen to pieces and then started trashing the house.

"He was looking for something," Ignacio said. "He kept saying, "Where is it? Where is it?" but every time Miguel or I would say, "What? What do you want?" he would look at us like we were crazy and say, "You don't even know! None of you even knows!"

Miguel added, "And we couldn't get him to stop trashing your room."

"He said you must have stolen 'it,'" Ignacio said.

"What did you steal, Esme?" asked Miguel.

"I didn't steal anything," I cried, running down the hall to see the damage.

"Well, Uncle sure thought you did," Ignacio called after me.

The violence done was so extreme, it made me afraid to even step through the door of my room. Furniture had been hurled higgly-piggly, drawers had been upended, my clothes wadded and rended in piles. Pictures were ripped from the walls, boxes pulled from the closet, the contents of my bookshelves swept to the floor.

"He was really pissed," said Miguel from behind me.

I turned to my brothers. They had followed me, and stood together in the hallway, shoulders touching, like small boys.

I took a deep breath, steadying my voice. "Where did Uncle Oscar go?"

They looked at one another and shook their heads. "We don't know."

"Did he drive?"

Again they looked at one another. Ignacio nodded. "He took the truck," he admitted reluctantly.

Miguel added quickly, "We couldn't stop him, Esme."

More than anything I wanted to curl in the hallway with my hands over my head and scream into the carpet. Instead, for the sake of my brothers, I swallowed my fears. "I don't know about you guys," I said out loud. "But I don't feel safe here. Not one bit." I pulled out my cell phone. "We should go."

"Where?" asked Miguel.

I spoke while I pressed buttons. "Annie has a bunk-house on her farm. It's only got a wood stove, and we'll have to run into the house to use the bathroom, but I like it better than this place right now."

"Can we bring the Xbox?" asked Miguel.

I gave him what I hoped was an arch look while I listened to Annie's phone ring. I heard the answering service pick up. My heart sank.

"Well? Is she answering?" Ignacio asked.

"No," I said. I added, deciding quickly, "But it's okay. Get some things together—please, not the Xbox, okay? Just what you'll need for this weekend—"

"What about Uncle Oscar—" Ignacio started to object.

I pointed over my shoulder at my room. "He's not in a safe head space and I don't know what he'll do next," I said, my voice thickening with tears. "I don't want to stay here, Ignacio. Go get your things."

Miguel and Ignacio turned and headed to their room. It's a testament to exactly how frightened my brothers were that they did what I said without any more discussion. I considered picking through the piles of my belongings and shrugged it off. The mess was too much like the muddle of feelings in my heart and mind; I couldn't even begin to sort it through.

Miguel and Ignacio soon emerged from their rooms dragging hastily packed duffel bags. "Aren't you packing anything?" Miguel asked.

"I can borrow Annie's stuff," I said shortly. I gestured down the hallway. Dragging their duffels, my brothers followed me out of the house.

It was cold and very dark outside. Stars sparkled above the trees. A pack of coyotes howled in the distance, sounding for all the world like a bunch of lunatics laughing themselves to death.

"Shouldn't we leave Uncle Oscar a note?" Ignacio asked.

I shook my head, shivering. "Let's just get out of here." The trees seemed too close and too dark. I thought about demons in the orchards and I slammed into the car. Ignacio and Miguel followed suit. I fired up the engine, flipped on my headlights and started driving down the dirt road.

Annie's land is five miles from our house and it is all orchards in between. My brothers were unnaturally quiet as my little car eased through the ghostly rows and flicking shadows. "Can you put on the radio or something?" Ignacio asked finally. "This is super creepy."

His hand reached for the dial but I slapped it away. I heard something strange outside the car. "What's that?" I asked.

"What?"

"Listen."

I strained my ears. There was the hiss of my tires on gravel, the growl of the engine and… something else. Something big. "I hear it," said Miguel from the back seat. I looked in the rearview mirror at his wide, brown eyes.

It sounded like a distant, crackling roar. I thought of a train rushing by; then I thought of a fire raging. Miguel said, "It sounds like Call of Duty," and my mind jumped to an army advancing down the dirt road.

"What the hell?" Ignacio had finally heard it too.

"It's getting closer!" Miguel said.

I clenched my teeth, resisting the urge to speed up. Rushing on dirt and gravel, I could easily lose control of the car. But the sound kept getting closer and closer, louder and louder. The dashboard vibrated. I pictured a giant bulldozer, a volcanic eruption, an earthquake. I gripped the wheel until my knuckles blanched, my palms slick with sweat.

"Let's get out of here!" Ignacio yelled.

I gave in. "Hang on!" I screamed and floored it.

It was a stupid, stupid thing to do. I am not an expert driver and my car was not a tank. We jounced, screaming and yelling, while the headlights jiggled crazily and the orchard jumped around us. Miguel's head struck the ceiling and Ignacio crashed into me.

"Put on your seatbelts! Idiotas!" I shrieked at my brothers.

They fumbled with the belts, still bouncing like popcorn in a kettle. My teeth rattled. The engine howled. A tidal wave of sound engulfed us.

I suppose it was inevitable. One of my wheels hit a rock and the car shot to one side. It seemed to happen fast and slow, all at the same time. The car, heading inexorably for a tree, Ignacio's body jerking forward over the dash, the impact and tearing sound of the front end hitting, the airbags unfurling in front of me and my chest and face smacking painfully. Then it was over.

"Are you guys okay?" I asked after a moment.

"I bit my lip," said Miguel.

"I'm think I'm here," groaned Ignacio.

We realized all at once that it had gone quiet. In the silence, our ragged breathing was very loud, as was the tick of the car's engine.

"Where are we?"

"Will the car still go?"

I tried the ignition. It turned over a few times, and then stopped.

"I think I totaled it," I whispered.

I felt sick. The front end had crumpled. The headlights tilted crazily; light shot off in different directions. The deflated airbag puddled in my lap, smelling of plastic. I unbuckled my seatbelt and wrenched open the door, thinking I might vomit. I heard Miguel gasp from the back seat. He stared out the windshield, eyes huge in his pale face. Trembling, I followed his gaze.

My first thought was of Paco Fernandez. He had called it "the devil on his horse," but it was a monster, pure and simple. In the cockeyed light of my car's broken headlamps I saw mostly teeth, white and glistening, each of them as large as my forearm, and stuffed in a vast maw as big as the windshield. A huge, misshapen hump erupted from its back; breath bubbled through its slimy nostrils. I remember eyes as big as snow tires, glowing with baleful green light. Its shadow lurched on the ground, as the thing swung its enormous body to face us.

"Get back in the car, get back in the car," Ignacio screamed at me while Miguel just yelled, "Esme! Esme!"

I have no memory of getting back in the car, but somehow I was there, my heart beating in my ears, my whole body bathed in sweat. I could hear Miguel sobbing as we watch the thing lumber towards us, opening its impossible jaws, steam pumping out of its nose in regular columns as it breathed. I remember thinking it came from somewhere else, where the air must be thicker, the gravity must be different, because it moved with an alien, heart-jittering swiftness, that seemed utterly wrong for this world.

"Do—Do you—think it—will eat—the car?" Ignacio's voice was hoarse and gasping.

I really did think it would eat the car, in fact, but my throat had closed around my voice box like a fist around a flower. Mute, I waited for the thing to begin eating its way into us.

"Should we run?" Miguel squeaked.

I couldn't answer. The monster's breath fogged the windshield. Its jaws brushed the headlights; we took in a heart-stopping glimpse of its glistening throat. I felt Ignacio's cold hand grip mine. Miguel's arms encircled his brother from behind. We hung like that, motionless, for what seemed an endless unspooling of time, waiting to be devoured. Then suddenly the creature turned, and slipped away into the shadows.

We sat breathlessly expecting its imminent return. But nothing happened. Then Ignacio said, "What was that?" and Miguel said, "Oh, God. I gotta pee."

Impossibly, we snorted with laughter as Miguel fumbled with his seatbelt and slid across the car seat.

"Wait," I said. "Don't go outside." I peered through the trees, seeing something else coming through the shadows.

"Oh, what now?" moaned Ignacio, all laughter snatched from the air.

"Hold on. I don't think it's the… the thing," I said. "It moves differently." I leaned forward peering into the dark. In the light of the headlamps I glimpsed a flash of white. Then the figure resolved itself in the gloom. "Oh, thank God," I said. "It's Fitzsimmons! Or Blob!"

"Who?"

I jumped out of the car. "Annie's dogs!" I wept with relief. "Annie's dogs are here to save us."

11.

Annie told me later that Fitzsimmons and Blob had both escaped their kennel and run away—unheard of behavior for her well-trained animals. She and Fluff had been chasing them in the truck when I phoned her, which was why she hadn't picked up. But the dogs led her straight to my crashed car. So shortly after Fitzsimmons and Blob appeared at the scene of the crash, Annie's truck rumbled up as well.

I explained to her a little of what had happened with my uncle and why were out in the orchards in the middle of the night. Neither my brothers nor I wanted to talk about the monster—or whatever we had seen. I just told her that I had driven too fast and lost control of the car. She nodded grimly, patted my brothers kindly, and loaded us, the giant dogs and all of our stuff in her truck without a murmur.

Once we were easing down the dirt road again, she said, "I imagine after the thing with your uncle and crashing your car, you've all got quite a bit of adrenaline in your systems."

"You think?" I said, bubbling with nervous laughter. I could not stop shaking, whether from relief or fear. My teeth chattered and my whole body periodically convulsed. I glanced in the back of the truck where each of my brothers huddled with one of the dogs. "We're—we're pretty freaked out."

"Well, you're all going to get incredibly irritable unless we can work the stuff out of your system. Especially the boys." Annie's wry practicality cut through my jittering laughter.

"Um, okay. What do you suggest?" I said meekly.

She said. "The bunk house is going to need some TLC to make it habitable. There's firewood to move, a lot of boxes to switch up, bedding and so forth to get out of storage. It's dark and it's cold and none of you are going to want to do this, but it's important that you throw yourselves into it. The most beneficial thing you can do after a big scare is work hard. Can you explain that to the boys?"

"Yes," I said. I swallowed and added, "Annie, something really awful's happening in Mattawa."

She said, "You mean the Fernandez murder—or whatever it is?"

"I mean… I mean you and I have to talk. Something… something really weird is going on. With me." I started to shake again uncontrollably.

She nodded, her glasses glinting in the blue lights from the dashboard. "Okay," she said. "But first, let's get your brothers settled, all right? I'll make some dinner. You guys get to work."

❄

Annie hadn't lied. A lot of work had to be done to get the bunkhouse in order. My brothers did not object. Having grown up in an orchard, they knew all about hard work, and they set about stacking storage boxes, sweeping cobwebs, mopping floors, and bringing in armloads of firewood without a single word of reproach. After an hour or so of vigorous labor, we had three bunks cleared, fresh bedding on each, a dust free sleeping space and a crackling fire in the Franklin stove. Annie fed us chowder and fresh bread in her kitchen. Through it all,

Blob and Fitzsimmons stuck by Miguel and Ignacio, padding beside them like giant, white, watchful nannies.

"They've decided you kids are part of the herd," Annie said to my brothers. "They're making sure you don't wander off like lambs."

"Can they stay in the bunkhouse with us?" Miguel asked, looking eight years-old, instead of fifteen.

Annie chuckled and said, "I don't know that I can stop them. Fluff is ready to whelp, so she'll stay in the house with me. But Fitz and Blob can stay with you, if it'll make you happy."

Ignacio and Miguel seemed very happy and relieved to have the gigantic dogs sleeping in the bunkhouse. Shortly after dinner, they began yawning. Annie had unearthed a DVD player and spare television from somewhere upstairs, and the boys enthusiastically set it up by the wood burning stove in the bunkhouse. They went off to their beds with a collection of disks—I noticed they did not select a single horror movie—the two big dogs in tow, all prepped to settle in for an Indiana Jones marathon.

"I don't know how to thank you for this," I said to Annie when the boys had left in a noisy jumble of big feet, big paws and big yawns.

"Think nothing of it," she said. "You're practically family." She shifted in her chair and asked, "Have you called your uncle?"

"I'm afraid to," I admitted and added, "If you saw our house, you'd be afraid too, Annie. It's… really bad."

She asked, "Would you like me to call him?"

I shook my head. "This is going to sound strange, but I don't want him to know where we are." I took a deep breath, deciding to get down to it. "Annie," I said. "I'm more scared than I know."

"Go on," she said quietly. "I'm listening."

I told her almost everything. She listened without comment. At one point, she got up and poured us both brandies. "I know you're not twenty-one for a week," she said. "But consider this a medicinal necessity."

Then she sat by the propane fire, eyes trained on the flames, while I went on in between burning sips. I told her about meeting Paco in the orchard. I told her some of what I had dreamed. When I told her about how the Strong Tea Woman had shown up at the Fernandez house, Annie shifted a little in her chair. When I got to the part where Miguel and Ignacio and I all saw the monster in the orchard, her eyebrows shot up. I finished by saying, "I know I should call a tow for my car, and call Mr. Olstein about the crash on his road, but I don't want to go out there in the dark, Annie. I'm too scared. If you had seen what we saw…" I trailed off. "What is it?" I asked. "Mass hypnosis? Poison in the water? What would make my brothers and me and Paco Fernandez all see the same horrible vision?"

Annie stared into the flames for a while and then cleared her throat. "Has it occurred to you that maybe there's actually a monster out there?" she asked.

"And I suppose Blob and Fitzsimmons scared it away?" I held up my brandy glass. "How many of these have you had?"

She grunted. "I'm just abiding by Occam's razor. The simplest hypothesis is usually the correct one." She added, only half joking, "Don't underestimate the power of Fitzsimmons, either. I sometimes suspect he's something of a shaman."

"Please. A shaman dog and an actual monster in the orchards is not the simplest hypothesis, Annie. It's just the craziest."

She pushed her glasses up her nose. "Did you see a monster?"

"Yes."

"And your brothers, too?"

"Yes."

"And Paco Fernandez?"

"…Yes."

"Well, that's four people. Four sane people. What else am I supposed to think?"

That I'm not sane, I thought as Annie got up from her chair.

"I need another brandy," she said with a wry smile. "I don't know about you, but I haven't had too many. After tonight, I'd say I haven't had enough."

I held my glass out and she took it. She paused at the kitchen counter, the brandy bottle in her hand, her sharp face grim.

"I've been living in this area for a long time, Esme, and it can be a pretty strange place. There's stories in Tieton, right down the road, of spirit lights and alien abductions. I heard a girl tell me, in all seriousness, that she found a werewolf skeleton buried in the trees, once." She nodded and poured a measure of brandy into each glass. "It's a strange place, hon. Back in the Sixties, when I first moved here, all us hippies were buying land by the river and trying to assimilate with the Native American tribes. And there was a lot of talk about skinwalkers in the hills back then."

"Skinwalkers?" I asked, as she handed me a small glass of amber liquid.

"Shape shifters," Annie said. "Put a demon and a vampire and a werewolf together and you come up with a skinwalker, more or less. Like a magician, but worse. More like a demon, I guess. Indians say they can look just like a regular person, but then they change into a monster at night. Gave me the willies every time I heard the coyotes, I tell you." She shuddered, sipped and went on. "That Midwinter Bonfire Festival we have every year? I helped start that tradition, back in the day. It's a Lion's Club thing now, to raise money for the Food Bank, and it's gotten very staid and family friendly, but when I was young? It had a lot more in common with a pagan fertility ritual. We made the fire burn all night to call the sun back from the edge of the earth—and sometimes I really felt like we were calling something else from the ground. Calling something to protect us." She laughed shortly. "You can say I might have been on drugs, and maybe I was. It was a different time. But I can remember more than a few midwinter nights, when I'd see things in the dark, and they didn't look too friendly. And I don't think it was the pot I smoked. I think I saw things that were… real."

"So you're saying there's a—what?—a skinwalker in Mattawa?"

"I know there's things in the world that aren't exactly of the world." She tipped her head back. "You know, the town elders and the old families in Ellensburg nearby—staid, salt of the earth white people, not Indians or Mexicans, or even hippie kids, I'm talking about people who pay their taxes, go to barbers and drink martinis—" she snorted "—even they get together every summer for a secret ritual in the woods. Really. They get drunk and dress one of the men up like a woman, and make fun of her and degrade her—like some bizarre echo of a human sacrifice. They might not remember why they do it—but mark my words, they wouldn't think of skipping it. Because they're protecting themselves, too."

"Protecting themselves..."

"From the monsters, the skinwalkers, the bad juju. The land here has power, Esme, and people who work the land have to nourish and harness that power, see that it doesn't fall into the wrong hands. The wrong hands exists, we all know it. The wrong hands in this world and the wrong hands in the world beyond."

"But why would there be a monster here now? And why would it come after me?"

Annie snorted. "I don't know, Esme. Maybe Fitz can tell you that one."

We were silent for a while, sipping our brandies and staring into the flames. Then Annie cleared her throat and said, "I actually had something I was going to show you. But right now, I'm not sure it's a good idea."

"Why not?"

"It's about your memory, Esmeralda. Or your lost memories."

I sat forward eagerly in my chair. "What did you find?"

Annie crossed the room to her laptop. She picked it up and placed it in my lap. She said, "One of the reasons I run a small town newspaper, is because I feel like I'm recording history. Someone wants to know what was going on in Mattawa in fifty years? I will have the answer; that's my service to the community I love." She leaned over me and tapped the keyboard. "I had you put thirty years of my issues online when I hired you and neither one of us noticed this article. Remember how I said I did a story on Christmas legends once? Well, look at this one. And look at the picture. And the name."

The article headline on the screen read, "Local Children Raise Money, Awareness With Christmas Legend." I squinted at the picture of a little girl and a little boy beaming by a row of potted plants. The caption read, "Esmeralda Ulloa and Xavier Sandoval and their classmates have raised almost $500 with their poinsettias."

I felt my skin contract into gooseflesh. "I don't believe this," I whispered.

Annie said, "You publish a paper a week for thirty years and the stories just blend together. This one was almost fifteen years ago, Esme. I forgot about your 'Flowers of the Holy Night.' Do you recognize your little friend, Xavier?"

"It's him," I breathed. I let my finger hover just over the screen. "It's who I dream about." *It's who I kissed today. It's who my uncle said he didn't recognize.* "He's real. He's really real." *Maybe I'm not crazy.*

Annie nodded. "You don't remember being in my paper when you were six years-old?"

"None of it," I peered at the picture, feeling my stomach go all hollow with helplessness. "I don't remember any of this at all."

She pushed a few more buttons on the keyboard and brought up another picture. "Do you remember this?" she asked.

The photo was of me, in a tight, black velvet dress I remembered very well from high school. I was wearing high, furry boots and tights. I beamed, clutching the hand of the boy Xavier again, a much old Xavier this time, tall and also obviously happy, his hair a little long, hanging in his eyes. The newspaper caption read, "Esmeralda Ulloa and her date, Xavier Sandoval are all dressed up for the Midwinter Fire Festival."

Annie said, "I remember that very well, actually. I was covering the Festival for the paper and I just had to take a picture of you both, even though you were a couple of kids. You had this radiance about you. It was like seeing a midwinter Romeo and Juliet. Young love in all its glory."

I looked at my happy face, the way we tightly we held hands. "This is my dream," I said.

"Part of it."

"It's not stars we're dancing in, it's all the Christmas lights and decorations for Midwinter Fires."

"Yes, I think so."

"He was my date for the Midwinter Fires Festival in ninth grade," I looked wonderingly at Annie. She nodded. "Well, what in the hell happened to him? And how did I forget that?"

❄

From the Mattawa Weekly News, November 27, 1996

LOCAL CHILDREN RAISE MONEY, AWARENESS WITH CHRISTMAS LEGEND

By Annie Mortmain

There is an old Mexican legend that the poinsettia came into existence when a little girl named Pepita, too poor to give something magnificent to the Christ child at a Christmas Eve services, presented Him with a handful of roadside weeds, which subsequently transformed into a beautiful flower. These "Flores de Noche Buena" or "Flowers of the Holy Night," otherwise known as poinsettias, are for sale a Wahluke Elementary School through December 21st, to help raise money for the local food bank.

"We were casting around ideas for a community fundraiser as a school project and Esmeralda Ulloa and Xavier Sandoval suggested poinsettias," said Wahluke teacher Elodia Miravel. "Until they told me the story, I was not aware of the Mexican Christmas legend."

Many of the poinsettias for sale have been locally grown in greenhouses attached to Olstein Orchards, where Esmeralda's uncle, Oscar Ulloa, is manager. Others have been ordered from companies outside of Mattawa, for sale at the school. So far, the children in Wahluke Elementary have raised $500 for the food bank.

Esmeralda Ulloa, a second grader, says she helps her uncle Oscar grow plants at Olstein Orchards "all the time." She and Xavier Sandoval, in fifth grade at Wahluke, both say they are happy to be selling plants at Christmas to help the poor. "I like growing things," said Esmeralda. "And spending time in my uncle's greenhouse just feels good."

For more information about buying a poinsettia for the fundraiser, contact the Wahluke School at the number below. There will also be a special poinsettia table at the Holiday Bazaar in Desert Aire on December 5th.

12.

In my dream, Uncle Oscar came to me with one of his carved, wooden boxes in his hands. He held it out. He said, "I'm sorry about this, Esmeralda. I didn't mean to have it turn out this way."

"Turn out what way?" I asked.

He shook his head. He said, "It can't do me any good where I'm going." He thrust the box in my hands. "I hope this helps. Take care," he whispered and turned away. "Whatever you do, don't follow me." His boots left no marks in the dust as he walked away.

I realized I stood on a red desert road, in full sun, with nothing but sage and scrub spreading out from either side for miles. I thought I might run after my uncle, but he had disappeared down the road, leaving only ripples of heat in his wake.

I stood, not knowing which direction I should turn. "Don't follow me," he had said. So at last I started walking on the road in the opposite direction, carrying the box in my hands. Little purple flowers sprouted at my feet as I walked, making a path of blossoms before and behind. They withered in the burning sun and filled the air with fragrant smoke. I turned the box over and over in my hands. Finally, I opened it. It was full of dust. The wind picked up and it started to blow away. I snapped the lid closed.

I heard hoof beats behind me and turned. A man on horseback trotted down the road from the west. The setting sun made a long shadow in front of him. More shadows obscured his face. I hoped he was Xavier. But as he grew closer, I saw it wasn't him at all.

"Give me the box and I'll take you for a ride," Justin Colter said, pulling up beside me on the road.

He sat on top of an enormous black horse, snorting and rolling its eyes. The noise of its breath reminded me of something unpleasant, but I pushed the thought away because Colter looked so delightfully handsome high above me, his face a little shadowed by his hat brim, his blue eyes very bright. His sensual mouth quirked, and I felt my own lips lift in response. "You won't just give me a ride?" I asked. "I have to give you something for it?"

"Always," he said lightly, like it was a joke.

I laughed. "Yes, all right," I said. "This is nothing anyway." I handed him the box full of dirt.

"This is exactly what I wanted, Esme," he joked, before tucking the box away in his saddle somewhere. For a second, I felt a little sad, seeing it disappear, like I had let something go that might be very, very valuable to me. But then that feeling was wiped from my mind as Colter held out his arm and then swept me in the saddle behind him in one impossibly strong, fluid movement.

He clicked his tongue and the gigantic beast underneath him began to lumber forward. I pressed myself up against Colter's broad back, feeling the saddle rocking between my legs. I was immediately, almost painfully aroused.

Colter's smooth voice rumbled, "I have what I want; you get what you want. Fair trade?"

"But I don't know what I want."

"Oh, yes you do."

A delicious friction had begun to build between my thighs, and I found

I did want something very badly. I pressed my palms to Colter's hard stomach, feeling a ripple of laughter deep inside him. The horse picked up speed, sending shocks of pleasure jolting through my core. "Yes," I whispered. "Oh, yes. And please don't stop."

He chuckled. "Enjoy the ride."

With each hoof beat, my nipples brushed against his shirt, until they swelled like tight little grapes, bursting on the vine. My skin flooded with warmth; my lips tingled. Colter whispered something in a rough voice, and the horse went even faster. I stroked myself against the saddle, maddened with both pleasure and frustration. I pressed my mouth to Colter's back. "More," I whispered.

"You can have it," he said. "Just stop saying, 'no.'"

"Yes," I moaned, stroking faster.

"Yes," he said and by then his voice had deepened into a growl. He didn't even sound human.

I couldn't hear hooves clopping underneath me anymore, only a kind of sinister rasping. I knew he had changed into something unspeakable. I knew that the beast we rode on was the stuff of nightmares. But I wanted him anyway, and I shut my eyes tight so I wouldn't have to see what he had become. I shut my eyes and rocked against him, biting my lip until blood ran down my chin, grasping for sweet pleasure that stayed always, always just out of my reach.

❄

I woke up with my heart pounding, terrified and aroused at the same time. At first, I didn't know where I was. Then I saw the glow of the Franklin stove and the white, furry shapes of Blob and Fitz, flopped on a rag rug by the fire. I heard my brothers' soft breathing and I remembered we were in Annie's bunkhouse.

Annie had lent me pajamas before I went to bed. I wrapped a sleeping bag around my shoulders and rose. The dogs raised their heads as I passed. They did not seem inclined to follow me outside. Fitz yawned and put his big head back on his paws. I took this as a sign that all was well on the farm, and that no monsters lurked outside the bunkhouse.

On the porch I pulled on a pair of boots before hiking up the hill and letting myself in Annie's big, warm house to use the restroom. Annie decorates with lots of color—the walls splashed with yellow and orange, a patchwork of rag rugs dotting the floors, bright red kitchen countertops gleaming, blue hangings festooning the walls. She had tiled the bathroom in turquoise and black and put yellow towels on the racks. I blinked at my reflection in the bathroom mirror. I looked like a woman caught in a Zapotec mosaic, an ancient Mexican goddess, surrounded by turquoise, with eyes of jade.

Back outside with the sleeping bag still wrapped around my shoulders, I watched dawn streak the sky. I considered going back in the house and making coffee, but I saw movement by the goat shed and found myself walking down there instead. A light coating of frost covered the sagebrush. The dawn made everything rosy.

I wasn't surprised to see him there, sitting on the steps of the shed, looking out at the fields of sage and grass, the big Columbia River a streak of distant silver. I hung back, a little shy in my pajamas and snow boots. Then I said his name, the only thing I really knew about him for sure. I said, "Xavier." He turned and smiled at me, getting to his feet. I could see him clearly in the pink light. I said, "Aren't you cold out here?"

He shook his head as I drew closer. "I don't get cold," he said. He put out his hand and I took it.

His palm felt warm, as if he had just held it against a mug of steaming tea. Even standing a few feet away from him, the heat from his body was tangible. "You've always been warm," I whispered.

He nodded. "You're remembering."

"I don't know what I'm remembering," I said. I looked into his dark gray and gold eyes, so strange and familiar all at once. "Is this another dream?"

He shrugged. "It will seem that way until you wake up, my love."

"But I am awake."

"Are you?" He smiled and I smiled back. He gestured to the steps and I sat, wrapping the sleeping bag around me. He sat next to me. I was excruciatingly aware of his shoulder brushing mine, the way his black hair flopped over his cheek. I knew that he had small ears. I knew a scar marred his left thumb, from cutting it on a sharp trowel years ago. I knew playing soccer in high school had made his thighs iron hard. I knew his heart beat a little faster, just because I was next to him, the same way my heartbeat had gone up a notch, like a little switch inside me had been flipped. I caught my breath as he eased one of his impossibly warm arms around my shoulder. The heat seeped deliciously into my skin. "What do you remember today, preciosa?" he asked.

"What I remember, and what I know are two different things," I said slowly. "I know I've known you forever," I said. "I know… I know we were friends as children… and then we were more than friends, as we got older. I think… you were the first boy I ever kissed. Is that right?"

"I would hope so," he said, his mouth soft as he smiled. "You were ten years-old."

I laughed but I felt tears building in my throat and burning my eyes. "You kissed me in the orchard. I dared you to do it." A memory flicked by, the orchard in bloom, heavenly scents, the thrum of bees in the blossoms.

"I wanted to, I promise—" his laughing face, so close to mine.

"And then I said you had to marry me—" his lips had been a little dry, but thrilling, his breath sweet in my mouth.

"I pretended to be mad about that—" outrage blooming in my chest.

"So I smacked you one—"

"Right on the mouth I kissed you with—"

"I was so angry—"

"You were really cute. I liked making you mad."

I didn't know if I was laughing or crying. My voice clogged on my ragged breath as I said, "Xavier. How old was I when Uncle Oscar made you go away?"

He stopped smiling. "You were fourteen."

"Right after the Midwinter Fires?"

"Yes." His voice sounded thick as well.

"Why? Why did he make you go?"

I felt his arm tighten on my shoulder. He said, "It will come to you."

"Did you do something bad?"

His mouth hardened. "I didn't. But someone might tell you I did."

I didn't want him to be angry. I cast around for something else to talk about. I saw he wore a leather bracelet on one of his wrists. Old and worn, the leather had frayed and cracked around the silver buckle. I touched it gently with my finger. His breath caught. "That thing's about to rot off your arm, you know," I said with a smile.

He sighed and smiled back a little sadly. He said, "I hope not."

"It's gross, you know."

That made him laugh. The moment of anger was gone. "It was a present from someone I used to know. It's not gross to me."

I watched sunlight spread on the scrubland in front of us and shivered, in spite of his warm arm.

"Where have you been all this time?"

He hesitated, then said lightly, "Laboring until you could come back to me. Learning my trade, the way you should have been learning yours."

"I'm getting an English degree, I'll have you know. I just finished a test about American mythology."

"Yes. You're trying to remember who you are." Idly, he reached down and broke off a stem of lavender, brown and withered from the cold. "Watch this," he said. He blew his breath on it and the stick burst into flames, like a little torch. He dropped it on the frozen ground where it burned, giving off sweet smoke.

"Are you a dragon?" I asked, only partly joking. "Like Quetzacoatl?" I added, thinking of the feathered serpent I had just studied about for my test.

He gave me a sharp look out of his gray eyes and reached down, breaking off another branch. "No. Not Quetzacoatl. Now you." He handed the stick to me.

"Now me, what? You want me to light this on fire?"

He shook his head. "That's not what you do," he said. His arm squeezed my shoulder. "Do you trust me?"

I turned the dead branch in my hands. I looked into his face. "What do I do?"

"Blow on it and see"

I blew on the stem and watched it turn green and then burst into purple flowers. It was like watching a stop motion film, only I could smell the leaves and the fresh clean scent of lavender blossoms. I laughed with wonder as little purple flowers rained on the step we sat upon. The wind picked them up and blew them around the frost-covered ground.

"Doesn't matter if its Ashmead Kernals, corn or poinsettias. Or lavender flowers. This is you. Just like the fire is me." He suddenly kissed my cheek and nuzzled my ear. "Wake up, preciosa. Before you get stolen again. Please?"

"I don't want to wake up from this," I said, as little tingles of pleasure shimmered down my neck and I turned the blossoming branch in my hands. "This is the best dream ever, Xavier."

"No, cara," he said, suddenly serious. His other hand reached for my shoulder, so he could turn me to face him. "You have to be more careful. Yesterday, I told you to choose, and you didn't. And now he is one step closer to having what he wants. And this is what he wants."

I pulled a little away. "What are you talking about?"

"Yesterday. Your uncle sat in his office and drank with the devil—"

"Justin Colter is just a vintner from Italy—"

"And the devil asked you what you wanted—"

"That was a casual conversation—"

Xavier shook his dark head. "No. There are no casual conversations with him, Esme. Every word he says is a trap."

"What are you talking about?" I thought back to yesterday afternoon, my uncle's office, the two of them sitting with their cups of cider. Colter's blue eyes twinkled up at me; Uncle Oscar gazed into his glass. Colter had said, *What do you want, Esme*?

"We were talking about college," I said to Xavier. "That's all."

"That's what he makes you think, every time," he said, voice cold. "That's how he always makes it seem. The stories have you signing a contract in blood, with this big ceremony, but really, he makes it seem like nothing, you understand? Like an afterthought. Like ordering a cheeseburger in a restaurant. When the whole time it's your soul you're giving away—"

"What are you saying?"

"I'm saying your uncle could have set you free, if you had asked. But now he can't help you—and I cannot either, not without your—"

I sat up, my sleeping bag slipping down. "What do you know about Uncle Oscar? Where is he?"

"He's gone, Esme. And you missed—"

"Where did he go—" I jumped to my feet.

Xavier ran a hand through his thick hair, standing. "It doesn't matter. He's gone. Listen. You have to listen, Esme. Do you understand? Because if you don't choose yourself—"

"No!" I cried. "I don't understand! I only know you come here and tell me what to do and I don't even know who you are!" I was suddenly furious. "Where did you go? Where did you go all this time and why did you leave me here all alone?" I put my hands on his chest to push him away, but he grabbed my wrists, his fingers so hot they seemed to burn into my skin.

"Nothing in this world kept me from you, I promise," he said. "And everything you do from now on will determine whether or not we can be together."

Faintly, I heard a dog barking on Annie's porch up the hill. He took a deep breath. "Esmeralda, listen. He will seduce you, he will scare you, he will throw distractions in your path. But you must keep trying to know who you are. You have everything you need to do this. Every single thing you need is right here, if you will see it. But you must work quickly. Because when midwinter comes it will be too late again, preciosa." He looked up the hill and muttered a curse. "I have to go," he said. "I don't know if I can come back. He'll get between us, now. He knows I am here."

"Xavier, wait," I said.

He brought his hands together and I saw him dissolve in a cloud of flames. Or maybe it was the sun rising in my eyes. The dog kept barking and barking.

13.

THE DEVIL AND HIS GARDEN
Part 2

The Devil made a garden and it crumbled into ashes. So he became very angry and stomped in circles, burning the earth, filling it with poisons. At last he tired of that, and cast about for some other way to grow fruit and flowers. For if the Devil could not make a garden grow on his own, then he would find someone to do it for him.

One day, the Devil saw a girl in an orchard. She was a magician's daughter and her name was Jardín. She had long, brown hair and eyes as green as grass. Wherever she went, the trees leaned in close and kissed her hands, the birds swooped from the sky and touched her fingers, the sun danced around her head in a halo of light. And the Devil thought, "If I steal Jardín for my own, I will have my garden, for she will nurture it."

So he made himself look like a beautiful lad, and he courted and pestered and called to Jardín, showering her with attention and gifts, until she turned her green eyes to him and smiled. Then he took her, but that was all, for the Devil only takes and he never gives anything in return.

Poor Jardín! The Devil built a high wall around her in the middle of the desert and said, "You belong to me now. Make me a garden."

At first Jardín refused, saying quite rightly that she belonged to no one but herself. But the Devil wove dreams, and the Devil told stories, and the Devil made it seem to Jardín that the world was very small indeed, something that really could be enclosed in four short walls, and that she was smaller still. And Jardín believed the Devil's lies, and forgot that she was anything but his slave. She whispered to the earth, and cried her tears upon it, and grew a garden only for the Devil. And the Devil was pleased, as he sat and watched his flowers grow. For though he could not make anything, he could weave a lie big enough to keep Jardín for his own. He enjoyed her beauty and he enjoyed her flowers and he enjoyed her tears most of all. For tears are like rain to the Devil; they fill his black heart with sharp, ugly blossoms of laughter.

14.

Colter's massive truck idled in Annie's driveway. Colter sat in the driver's seat, looking warily down at Fitz, who barked and growled like a furry demon. Colter waved when he saw me come around to the front of the house, still dressed in my boots and pajamas. He rolled down the window.

"That's quite an animal."

"He's Annie's," I said, above the barking. "What are you doing here?"

"Looking for you," he said. "I've been calling your phone since last night. Didn't you get my messages?"

I shook my head. I realized I hadn't seen my phone since we'd arrived at the house.

"Last night was a little intense. Quiet, Fitz," I said to the big white dog, who completely ignored me. I heard Fluff barking in the house, while Blob growled down the hill by the bunkhouse. "You'd better wait until Annie can call them off," I said.

Annie came out a short time later, bundled in a furry red robe and Uggs. She looked grimly up at Colter, as welcoming as a badger until he smiled down at her, and then I saw her visibly relax. While she ordered Fitz and the other dogs in the kennel, I hustled Colter in the cozy house and sat him by the stove. I thought about Xavier's warnings, but under Colter's bright blue gaze, that earlier conversation seemed as dim and insubstantial as a dream. Colter looked so incredibly handsome, sitting by Annie's propane fire, dressed in a cerulean chamois and jeans, his square hands resting on his knees, concern and affection creasing his face.

"I stopped by your house early this morning, Esme," Colter said. "After the way your uncle was, after I left him…" he trailed off, shaking his head.

"What about Uncle Oscar?" I asked.

Colter shifted in his chair. He said carefully, "I don't know how to say this, but your uncle became very agitated last night. I think it was my fault. I feel responsible, anyway. We were talking about you. I asked a lot of questions." He gave me an almost shy look from under his brows and a fleeting smile. "I'm a little interested in you. Maybe you've noticed."

By then, Annie was over by the counter fixing coffee, her gray-blond hair falling in her face and her glasses slipping down her nose. She snorted when she heard Colter's comment. He glanced at her. "Well, she's beautiful, and interesting," he said to her. Annie nodded and I felt myself blush.

"Anyway," Colter's gaze swept back to me. "I asked him about you, what you were like when you were a girl, what you were interested in. Stuff like that. He kept getting more and more restless and then he started pacing the room, saying he knew that guy in the picture you showed him. You know the one you thought you recognized?" I nodded. "Well, he said he'd lied about not knowing who he was. He said that guy was the spitting image of your cousin, Xavier."

"Cousin?" Annie asked.

"Xavier?" I said. I tried to sound casual as I said it, but my voice shrilled.

He nodded. "I guess you knew him when you were a kid? And you were very good friends?" His bright gaze seemed to probe mine. I simply swallowed and nodded, hoping he would say more. He went on, "Anyway, your uncle explained to me that you and Xavier had been very close, but as he saw it, this boy turned into a very nasty character as he got older. He was insecure, had control issues, whatever. He became deviant—started carrying guns and got into the occult. So your Uncle sent him away."

"Really?" Annie said.

"Oscar said the boy became very unstable when he entered high school and the older you got, the more he used feared for your safety. I guess he had a fixation with you, Esmeralda." Colter's eyes pierced me. "But surely you know all this?"

The coffee pot suddenly erupted into steam and bubbles. Annie quickly clattered mugs on the counter and poured. I said, "I guess I don't remember him that well. Xavier and I… We, uh, we must not have been as close as Uncle Oscar thought." I thought of Xavier's warm arms around me, about kissing him in the orchard when we were young, about talking to him only a few moments before in the pink light of sunrise. I hoped Colter wouldn't be able to tell I was lying.

"Ah, well," said Colter, smilingly accepting a mug of fragrant coffee from Annie, who padded over to us in her Uggs. "Anyway, here's where things got sticky yesterday. We were, ah, both on our third or maybe fourth bottle of cider by then." He ducked sheepishly. "That stuff packs quite a kick, doesn't it?" I nodded and Annie sniffed. "Anyway, I'd gotten pretty in my cups and felt ready for a nap. But Oscar gets more agitated. The idea that this bad kid might be back in town now—well, it sent your uncle into a rage, Esmeralda. I mean, I'd never seen anything like it. He worked himself into a froth and then he went tearing off in his truck like a bat out of hell. By then I was so tipsy, I could barely drive myself home. Somehow I did and I slept off the cider for a few hours. I woke up feeling terrible though, and started calling Oscar—and you, Esmeralda—to find out if everything was all right. When neither of you answered or called back, I decided to stop by your uncle's office, then his house this morning. I knocked on the doors. I looked in the windows—I was very worried—and I didn't like what I saw."

"My brothers and I didn't like it either. That's why we all decided to sleep here," I said.

"I hope nothing's happened to your uncle," Colter said. "Do you want some help looking for him?"

I nodded my head. "I would like that very much."

I meant it. I might no longer question whether or not Xavier existed. But now I wondered if I shouldn't be very afraid to see him again. Only my uncle would be able to tell me for sure. The sooner I could talk to him, the sooner I would know who—and what—Xavier really was.

❄

Shortly after that, my brothers wandered up from the bunkhouse. They ate bowls of cereal by the fire while I looked for my phone. I finally determined I must have left it at the scene of the crash the night before, and headed down to the goat shed to use Annie's office line to call a tow truck for my car. While I was there, I called Dane Olstein, who owned the tree I had crashed into, (along with the house I lived in and most of the land in Mattawa). I was embarrassed to tell him I had crashed my car on one of his orchard roads, but Olstein was very understanding. He asked me first if I was injured. When I told him I wasn't, he simply told me to tell my uncle which trees I'd run up against. As orchard manager, it would be Uncle Oscar's job to assess any damage that had been done. *If only I could find Uncle Oscar*, I thought to myself.

While I went through the motions of taking care of things, my mind zoomed in hyperdrive, speeding through what Colter had told me about Xavier. *Was Xavier really my cousin*? I had always thought my brothers and I were orphans. *And what was this business about Xavier being involved in the occult? Did that have anything to do with the monster in the orchards? With the murder of Paco Fernandez? He can burn things*, I thought, remembering the sprig of lavender in his hands. *And Paco Fernandez had been burned.*

By the time I hiked back up the hill to Annie's house from the goat shed, my neck and shoulders were rigid from stress. I had to consciously resist the temptation to grind my teeth and clench my jaw with worry. I found Colter and my brothers laughing by the fire, but their faces sobered as they all looked at me when I walked in the house.

"Here's the plan," I said. "I think at least one of us needs to be at home at all times today, so that we can intercept Uncle Oscar if he comes back. I need a ride down to my car—"

"Where's your car?" asked Colter.

"Long story," I said. I turned to my brothers. "Let's make a list of all the places Uncle Oscar might have gone to last night. Anywhere you can think of. Friends he might know. Places he liked to go. He could have crashed his truck the same way I crashed my car. He might need our help." *He could have run into a monster, too,* I added silently. I could see from my brothers' scared faces that they were thinking the same thing.

I turned to Colter and said, "Maybe you could take my brothers around Mattawa, once they come up with a list? I think I should stay at our house and see if my uncle comes home." *And that way, I can question him privately about Xavier if he does come home..*

Colter opened his mouth to say something, probably to voice an objection, but Miguel said, "Sweet! We get to ride around in that cool truck?" and Ignacio invited a high five. At that, Colter folded his lips shut. I was glad. Even with my whole body stiff from stress, his sexual magnetism tugged at all my senses. I knew I wouldn't be able to resist it, and I didn't want that distraction. I just wanted to clean up my house, find my Uncle Oscar, and settle once and for all who this Xavier was, and what his return to my life really meant.

"You need a car to get around, Esme," Annie said. She quietly scrubbed the crimson kitchen counter, her face carefully expressionless. "I can let you borrow the Holy Terror, if you like."

I laughed in spite of myself. Annie's "Holy Terror" is an ancient VW van she keeps stored on her property. Painted a wretched shade of school bus yellow, festooned with rust and actual bullet holes, the Terror is a relic from Annie's hippie days. She swore when it stopped running she would turn it into garden art, but thus far it refused to die.

"I would delight in riding the Holy Terror," I said with a mock curtsy.

"Take Fitz with you too," Annie said darkly.

I nodded and smiled while my brothers high fived again. If my uncle was angry, if the monster returned, if the mess was too much, Fitz would take care of me. "Thanks, Annie," I said out loud.

15.

Uncle Oscar's house still looked deserted some time later when I puttered up the driveway in the Holy Terror, Fitz imperturbably riding shotgun. We had met the tow truck in the orchard, and I had arranged to have my car repaired. I had retrieved my phone (it had been, as I suspected, discarded at the scene of the crash). Meanwhile, Miguel and Ignacio were sending me regular text updates from their odyssey around town with Colter. So far, they had not found Uncle Oscar, either.

"If we can't find him in the next twelve hours, I'm calling the police," I told Fitz. He waved his tail at me. I took it as a signal of approval.

By daylight, the mess in the house was even more depressing. If not for Fitzsimmons, who sniffed everything with enthusiastic interest, I might have closed the front door and sat on the porch to wait for my uncle. But Fitz kept up my spirits by wagging his tail, and picking up various things in his mouth to show to me. "Yes, that's a very nice wooden box, Fitz," I said, when he brought me a slobbery specimen, "Uncle Oscar made that. Please leave it alone." Or, "Yes, Ignacio really uses that smelly body spray. Maybe we should bury that, huh?" Or, "Wow, Fitz. Where did you find that Beanie Baby? Do you really want to keep it?"

In an hour or two I had the kitchen put to rights. Then Fitz and I moved on to my room, where the Uncle Oscar's hurricane of destruction had its epicenter. At first we merely stood on the doorway, staring at the chaos. Then Fitz picked his way in and began nosing through the piles. He looked up at me as if to say, "Shall we?"

"Yeah, okay buddy," I said.

I started filling large plastic bags with junk—a lot of it my papers and notes from school, but also broken vases, tangled costume jewelry, a cracked coffee cup or two, photo albums, old cards. Fitz found a comforter puddled on the floor and lay down, turning around first in a furry, white circle. While I worked, I talked to him, to keep up my spirits. He dozed and thumped his tail.

I had several bulging plastic bags of garbage to take out of the house to the dumpster by the time I was finished cleaning. It was afternoon by then and the sun sparkled on the trees, weaving a latticework of shadows on the frozen ground. Fitz ran off into the orchard, happy to be out of the house. I heaved my trash into the dumpster. My eyes were drawn to a patch of freshly overturned earth near a tree's roots. Carefully I flipped the dumpster's clanging lid closed and went over to investigate.

I smiled a little as I drew near. My uncle must have been reading my article about Apple Tree Man. He had started to dig a hole at the roots of one of the trees, and a little pile of apples—some of his finest heirloom ones, shiny skins bursting with health and color—sat near a spade.

It seemed sad to leave the rite unfinished. I knelt and took up the discarded spade, making the hole deeper and wider, so all of the apples would fit easily in it. The earth was very hard and I started to sweat as I chipped away at the frozen ground.

I heard a hollow thumping noise and realized an object was buried in the earth. I blew on my frozen, cramped fingers, rubbed my hands to warm them, then tried to feel the shape of what I had found by tapping and brushing at the dirt. Eventually, I pried loose another of Uncle Oscar's wooden boxes. I held it in my filthy hands and felt afraid.

Part of me wanted to bury it again without opening it. Whatever was inside, it was Uncle Oscar's secret. But curiosity got the better of me. I finished the ritual, placing the fruit in the hole and covering it, patting the earth down around the roots. By then, Fitz had returned from his wanderings. He sniffed the little box delicately and whined, deep in his throat.

"You don't like this either, do you?" I said to him. I left him, sniffing suspiciously at the freshly buried apples. I took the box into the house. I washed my hands at the kitchen sink and then sat at the table to open it.

16.

I opened the box and it felt as if a wad of moths had been loosed to flutter up and beat their wings inside my brain. My mind and then my whole body buzzed with panic and revulsion, as a hundred little memories swooped into my consciousness in a single, seething mass.

He held me in his arms. I could feel the silky skirt I wore floating around my thighs as we turned and turned. I knew everything about him. He had a little constellation of freckles on his neck in the shape of a cross; flecks of gold lightning decorated his storm gray eyes; he had a habit of tossing his head to get the long black hair out of his face. All around us other couples were dancing. Lights twinkled in the trees. In a clearing nearby, a gigantic fire burned. The air smelled of smoke, snow and caramel apples.

People from everywhere in town had brought things they no longer wanted to burn in the fire. They had written private sins and confessions on crumpled pieces of paper; they had brought old furniture they wanted to throw away and pictures of people they wanted to forget, hundreds of tokens of events or feelings they no longer wanted to remember. They had thrown all the refuse of the previous year in the fire so it would burn away.

The flames would burn all night, and when morning came, the year would be made new, and all the unwanted things wiped away.

Xavier held me close, rocking his hips against mine. "You know what the bonfire really is?" he whispered to me. His voice was husky and sounded strange in my ears.

I shook my head. He smiled a little knowing smile and swooped to my ear again. "It's magic," he rasped.

"No, it isn't," I said. "It's just for fun."

He indicated the lights and the fire, the dancing couples with a wave of his hand. "It looks all innocent, but it's really a kind of magic." He leaned in close, putting his mouth to my ear again. "I'm magic, too."

"What do you mean?" I asked, thrilling at the feel of his warm breath on my ear.

He whispered, "I can make things happen that would blow your mind, Esme. Do you want to see?"

The little shiver of pleasure became a silvery tickle of fear trickling down my spine. "No..." I tried to pull away from him. He grabbed me hard and his hands cut into the flesh of my arms. "Ouch, let go!" I cried.

"No, Esmeralda. You're mine," he growled. His hands burned into my flesh and I was suddenly very, very afraid.

❄

I slammed the lid on the little box. Annie had told me that repressed memories could suddenly be unlocked by a word, a smell, a sound. Somehow this little box had unlocked my mind. I shivered while a host of other horrid images washed across my memory like a wave of sewage. *Mutilated creatures found in the orchards. Xavier with a proud smile on his handsome face. My uncle's look of concern as I took Xavier's hand in mine. Xavier holding his palm aloft, and his fingers bursting alight like a row of candles. Xavier laughing at me, saying, "What? Do you think I sold my soul to the devil, or something, Esme?" My uncle, furiously angry; Xavier with a murderous expression on his face, saying to my uncle, "What makes you think you can keep her from me?" My uncle saying, "I will see to it that you will never have her!" And again, Xavier saying, "I can make things happen, Esme. Do you want to see?"*

Where I'd had no memories at all, suddenly I had hundreds, and they all had to do with Xavier, and every one was tainted with evil, like sticky black smoke stains on a freshly painted white wall.

My heart beat loudly in my ears. I could see why I had repressed everything that had to do with Xavier. He was pure evil. My uncle had been right to send him away.

But Xavier had told me I would hear bad things about him. He had told me they weren't true.

A memory of his madness, of his crazed face, zoomed into my mind. Of course he would tell me something like that. How else could I stand to be near him?

My chest contracted in fear. *Was Xavier a skinwalker*?

I remembered Annie mentioning Occam's Razor. *Here is a simple explanation: Xavier returns to Mattawa after a long absence. At the same time, a monster appears in the orchards. Xavier conjures flames. A man catches fire and dies in a ditch. And now I have these memories surface of murderous rages and horrible deeds...*

Fitz's barking startled me out of the wash of unwanted memories, questions and thoughts. It had grown darker; I had sat at the table for who knows how long. Headlights gleamed through the front windows. I rose and ran for the door, hoping my uncle had finally returned.

But it was Colter's black truck pulling into the driveway. My brothers were already climbing down from the cab as he shut off the engine. Fitz stood on the porch, growling and barking at Colter, the same way he had that morning.

"Is Uncle Oscar here?" Miguel asked.

"You didn't find him?" I said.

Ignacio shook his head and I could see Miguel visibly deflate. "We went everywhere," he said. "We even drove all the way to the casino and back."

"He didn't call you?" Ignacio asked. There was a plaintive note to his voice that made him sound very young.

"I can check my phone again, but I didn't hear anything." I turned to Colter. He looked as grim, pale and as discouraged as my little brothers. He stood back warily, eying Fitz, who still growled. I put a hand on Fitz's head to calm him. "Thank you for trying to find my uncle," I said. I added, "Can I make you some coffee, or something?"

"That would be nice," said Colter. He gestured at Fitz, still showing his teeth. "That dog really doesn't like me."

"He's trained to protect the lambs from the wolves," I joked. "He must just think you're a wolf."

"What can I do to change his mind?"

I said, "Just come in the house. Fitz can stay outside."

The little box still sat on the kitchen table. I picked it up and placed it on a high shelf before my brothers could comment on it. Quickly, I made coffee and set out some cookies. The boys were tired and subdued. They palmed a few cookies and soon went to their room; probably to lose themselves in the digital world, check up on football scores, Facebook, Twitter. It was Saturday night. I wondered if they would go out. After the brush with the monster—or whatever it was—they might want to stay home. But they might want to talk to someone. I know I wanted to have someone to talk to, very badly indeed. *Where had my uncle gotten to*?

I looked at Colter. He was so undeniably handsome, so readily helpful. Really, he looked almost angelic in the soft, warm kitchen light, his blond hair ruffled, his blue eyes tired. I noticed the gold hair on his arms, attractive smile lines in the corners of his eyes.

Colter caught me looking at him and smiled tiredly. "Has your uncle ever done anything like this before?"

I shook my head. I said, "Sometimes he blows off steam at one of the casinos, but mostly, really, he's just obsessed with his apples and his carving. I mean, as long as I can remember, all he has done is work on those heritage things and make little boxes from apple wood. And take care of us, of course."

Colter smiled. "Somehow I have a feeling you do a lot of the caring for this family, Esmeralda. Am I right?"

"Well, I'm the oldest," I said lightly.

"You're not that old. What are you, nineteen? Twenty?"

"I'm twenty-one," I said. "Almost. It's a few days until my birthday."

He shook his head. "You handle a lot of responsibility for someone so young."

"Farm kids are used to responsibility." I shrugged.

He nodded. I sat down across the table from him with my coffee cup. My hand rested near his and he reached out and covered it with his own. He said, "There's a lot going on for you right now, Esmeralda. I know you don't know me very well, but would you like to talk about it?"

I hesitated. There were so many things I wanted to talk about. I was afraid of so much. A feeling of helplessness swept me and before I could stop them, tears began trickling down my cheeks and huge sobs erupted from my chest. I heard Colter's chair scrape and an exclamation. I don't know how I got there, but suddenly I was in his arms, cradled in his lap, my face pressed to his soft chamois. His big hands caressed my hair, stroked my back; he murmured in my ear. I felt the heat from his body radiating to my core. Softly he began kissing my neck, my hands, the tears on my face. I was still weeping and trembling when his mouth came down on mine.

I felt the light touch of his lips, the barest whisper of contact. Immediately, explosively, my body flooded with hunger. Blood rushed to my face; my heart rate accelerated. "Oh, Esme," he whispered. I pressed myself to him and he gathered me in.

His kiss had begun as questioning and careful, but as soon as I kissed him back, his mouth responded, becoming more demanding. He sank his teeth into my bottom lip while his hands slid from my back to my hips. He pulled me forward, the better to grind his pelvis against my own. I felt him, rock hard through his blue jeans, and I began shuddering with desire. His fingers unbuttoned my blouse; my own flew to his chamois. I remember an awareness in some corner of my brain that what I was doing was inappropriate, wrong. It would solve nothing; it might complicate my life even further. But all the confusion, grief and fear demanded some kind of release. Colter was offering, and I was taking. He pushed my bra to the side and gently rubbed my nipples, teasing them into hot, tight peaks; I gasped, running my hands over his hard torso, letting my tongue dance with his, sucking greedily, even as the tears I had wept were still wet on my cheeks.

I don't know which penetrated first, Fitz's barking or the shrilling of my phone. But I pulled myself away from Colter, remembering my uncle. I scrabbled on the table, finding my phone, putting it to my ear. I was breathing heavily, and my heart slammed against my ribcage. "Hello?" I gasped.

The timbre of Annie's voice made me slither abruptly from Colter's lap and stand, weak-kneed, my bra askew, my blouse undone, hair hanging in my face. "Where are you, Esme?" she said.

"I'm at home." I leaned up against the table, looking at Colter, splayed in my kitchen chair, the blue shirt open, lips swollen from my kisses. Disgusted with myself, I turned my back, the better to listen to Annie.

She said, "You'd better come right away, honey. Something very bad has happened." And when she started to tell me about it, I forgot all about Colter for a time.

17.

Like any good small town journalist, Annie sometimes listens in on the local police band, which was how she heard about my uncle. She was in her truck and at the scene before the police had even identified his body.

I told the boys and Colter that I had to go out to help Annie with a story for the paper. The boys just shrugged. They were already mesmerized by their computer screens.

Colter was a little harder to shake off. He wanted to know what kind of story I was chasing, but I hedged. Annie's news about my uncle was like a bucket of filthy water thrown on a roaring fire. My ardor had died abruptly, leaving only the faint stench of shame and barely averted regret. I saw Colter to his truck without telling him anything. Fitz stayed in the house to guard my brothers.

At the police station, I functioned in a kind of fog. I received verification of my uncle's death from a distance. I felt outside myself. It was as if I had drifted into a story, maybe one from my recent classes on folklore or fairytales. *Once upon a time there was a little orphaned girl named Esmeralda Ulloa. She lived with her kind uncle and two brothers in an apple orchard. Her uncle grew magical fruits that kings and princes around the world coveted—apples of gold, apples of silver, apples with flesh that tasted of cinnamon and spices. And then a monster stole into the orchard one day and everything changed...*

The facts were horrifying. My uncle's body had been found on the banks of the Columbia River, some distance from town. The assumption was that he had died from drowning, but there was going to be an investigation.

"Is there something else I should know?" I asked the Mattawa Police Chief, Alex Sanchez.

We were still in the police station, bathed in the merciless flicker of florescent lights. Phones rang and doors swung; the smell of burnt coffee filled the air. Annie murmured softly to someone nearby, but I barely registered any of it.

Alex sucked on his thick mustache and shook his head. "I can't say, Esme," he told me. "The coroner is going to have to weigh in."

"Tell me what you know," I begged. "Please, Alex." As Annie's assistant, I had spoken to Sanchez in an official capacity multiple times. I had taken his picture, called him on the phone for statements. I considered him a friend. I said, "This is my Uncle Oscar we're talking about."

He hedged. "You've got a lot to do, honey. Don't worry yourself about all this until we know the whole story..."

"Just tell me... was he burned? Or-or—bitten?"

Immediately his eyes grew sharp and he looked at me closely. "What do you know?" he asked.

"I don't. But I was thinking of Paco Fernandez and wondering if the two deaths were similar. Or related." *Also, I saw a monster in the orchard last night*

Alex glared at me from under his brows. "We'll be investigating that," he admitted slowly.

"So he was burned," I heard my voice break. "Badly?"

"Do you know something about it, Esme?"

I hesitated and then said, truthfully enough. "A cousin of mine came back to town recently. His name is Xavier Sandoval. My uncle was worried about him." *He might be the skinwalker. He might have killed my uncle. And I think I'm still in love with him.*

Sanchez took a notebook and pen out of his shirt pocket and wrote down Xavier's name. "Do you know where I might find your cousin?"

I shook my head. I didn't tell him that as far as I knew, up until recently, Xavier Sandoval had only lived in my dreams.

❄

"I don't know what to do right now," I said to Annie a little later. We stood outside the police station. Snow had begun to fall, coating Mattawa's little main street with whispering sparkles. It was late at night by then and silence shrouded the town.

"Mr. Olstein's going to want us to move out of the house. He's going to have to hire a new orchard manager." My heart contracted in panic. "Where are we going to live? What am I going to do with the boys?"

"You can stay with me," Annie said firmly.

"In the bunkhouse? Until Miguel graduates? He's only a freshman and you don't have a bathroom." My voice had a hysterical edge that I couldn't hide.

"I'll build you a bathroom. Don't worry about that right now."

"It's just…" I trailed off, ashamed of my thoughts and feelings, which seemed incredibly selfish. *It's just that I don't think I can*, was part of it. *I think I'm going crazy*, was another. *I think I'm in love with a murderer*, was still another. *I don't know who to trust*, was yet one more.

But underneath those thoughts was a darker thought altogether and it was, *It's my fault Uncle Oscar is dead.* His death was mixed up with Xavier's return and Xavier had everything to do with me. I didn't want Annie's life put into danger, too. I didn't want my brothers hurt, either. "I don't know what I'm saying," I finally said, as helpless tears poured down my face for the second time that night.

"Oh, hell. Let's not make any decisions right now, then." Annie's thin arms went around me. "You want me to go home with you?"

I nodded. "I've got to tell the boys what happened. I don't want to be alone when I do that."

Annie said, "I'll stop by my house and get the brandy and the rest of the dogs."

"Thanks, Annie." I looked around me at the snow falling like cold little stars in the street. "Uncle Oscar always liked the snow," I said, my voice trembling. "It meant there would be a little vacation from all the farm work. He said only farmers and school children really appreciated the beauty of a snow day." Annie held me while the little stars swam in my eyes and warm tears streaked down my face.

❄

From the Mattawa Weekly News, December 14, 2012
Obituary: Oscar Everisto Ulloa

The Mattawa community is sorry to bid farewell to Oscar Everisto Ulloa. Born in Mexico, Ulloa immigrated to the United States as a youth, where he worked as a migrant farm worker in Southern California and Arizona, before moving to Washington with his three children in the 1990s. A long time resident of Mattawa, Oscar worked for twenty years for Olstein Orchards, fifteen of those as general manager. Under his leadership, Olstein's Fruit Company has become known as one of the world leaders of growing and preserving heritage apple varieties. Once widely grown in the United States from 1600 through the 1900s, heritage apples were hedged out of the market as small family farms in America gave way to corporate farming practices. Ulloa was a leader in the movement to bring flavorful, traditional heritage fruits back to the supermarket and to tables across America. "Oscar was a magician, plain and simple. I've never seen anyone grow fruit the way he could. He helped me brand this company as a leading cultivator of heritage apples," Dane Olstein, owner of Olstein Orchards said of Ulloa. His three adopted children, Esmeralda, Ignacio and Miguel Ulloa, all residents of Mattawa, survive Oscar Ulloa. A memorial service for Ulloa will take place On December 20, 2012, at Desert Aire at 10am.

18.

Grief is a little like being in a fresh snowfall. A light, cold curtain falls between you and the rest of the world. Simple things like opening your front door, walking down your front walk are suddenly more difficult. You slide unexpectedly into hurtful places. The earth seems to shift under your feet. You find yourself wanting to stay inside, hunker down. You stare out the window at a place you no longer recognize. It used to be your world, but now it belongs to the white, bleak cold.

When someone close to you dies, there's a million terrible little tasks, each more numbing than the next. Packing up belongings. Sifting through papers. Contacting lawyers. Contacting the IRS. Making more and more and more phone calls. I did those things, with Annie's help. But I was like a sleepwalker, going through the motions.

Dane Olstein gave my brothers and I until the end of January to clear out the house we had lived in, while he hired a replacement for my uncle. It was generous, under the circumstances. The boys and I divided our time between Annie's farm and the house we'd grown up in. School was out, and we used the time to sift through our belongings, packing up our things, even though I had not really decided where we would move. Annie did her best to involve us in the holidays—making the boys cut down a Christmas tree, insisting that we make buñuelos, whipping up pots of hot chocolate and ponche navideño, reminding us about the upcoming bonfire and dance. I think Miguel and Ignacio responded to her kind ministrations with joy and relief. But I felt swept up in a chaos of darkness.

Some events and images stand out from this time. One is going to the elementary school to collect "Letters to Santa Claus" from a classroom full of rambunctious second graders, to print in the *Mattawa Weekly News* for my column. I had set the date up weeks ago with the teacher at Wahluke School. The afternoon I spent with the children was a lovely oasis in the middle of a cold desert of grief. The letters they had written—illustrated and printed painstakingly in their best handwriting—lit a candle of laughter in my shrouded heart, if only temporarily.

Another vivid memory is going to the bank with my Uncle Oscar's safety deposit key. It was a week or so after his death. I was still mired in the middle of completing the endless tasks that a death in the family entails. My car still indisposed, I rode in the blatting and complaining Holy Terror—cold wind streaming through the bullet holes, making my skin feel coated with ice.

Warmth and quiet blanketed the inside of the bank. I had never opened a safety deposit box before. A clerk escorted me to an inner room and made me present identification as Uncle Oscar's heir and sign a ledger before I could open the box. She left me alone to see what it contained.

It held copies of the adoption papers for my brothers and myself, our birth certificates and Uncle Oscar's immigration and naturalization papers. Two of his small wooden boxes rested inside as well. I opened them and recognized the locks of brown-gold hair nestled inside. Uncle Oscar had saved my hair, but not my brothers'. I wondered why.

Mystified, I also drew out two small cloth bags with a number of oddities inside them—twigs, seeds, feathers, tiny stones. They reminded me of the spirit bags sold in tourist shops on nearby Native American reservations. These small pouches were supposed to provide the bearer with certain powers and attractions—wealth, love and good luck, for instance. You wore the bag around your neck and the small tokens created a little magic spell, like a lucky charm.

I thought it very odd that my uncle would have such things in his safety deposit box. He had never seemed like a very superstitious man. The secret locks of hair, the little bags of seeds, they made me feel hollow and strange inside, like I had not known him at all.

I also found a letter, written in Spanish, in a bold hand, on thick paper. Loosely translated, it read something like this:

"Oscar, by the time you get this letter I will have gone. Don't try to follow me. I want nothing to do with you or what you have chosen to do. This hurts me more than you will know, but in the interests of my own integrity and safety, and that of my grandson, I must remove myself from you and your actions.

"Oscar, you risk yourself and everything you hold dear by using the girl in this way. You will invite the attention of powers you do not want to associate with. Seven years is the customary term of service. You know this. To keep her longer is to invite your peril. They will notice. They will seek her out. The chances that they will find her before she is of age are very good indeed.

"You fool yourself by thinking you can keep her safe. You tell me you will erect a wall around her, but you do not have that much power, Oscar. Walls can be scaled and walls can be destroyed. Your pride will be your downfall, as it always is, as it always must be. Evil finds pride, Oscar. Pride is the magnet of evil.

"Beware, my friend. It is not too late to humble yourself and set her free. Remember me, even as I do what I can to forget you. Donna of the Saints."

The letter mystified me. I did not know any "Donna of the Saints." I did not know who she meant by "the girl," although I suspected she might be referring to me. But the most disturbing aspect of the letter was her intimation that my uncle had been a superstitious man, even one who believed in, or even practiced magic. Because I remembered him simply as a dull, dutiful farmer, obsessed by apple whips, root grafts, fruit.

Sitting in the little room in the bank, with its staid blue carpeting and hushed atmosphere, I felt very cold and alone. I had known my uncle to be a practical man, who made a living by putting his hands in the earth. But in this private place he chose to store a collection of tokens that indicated, at one time in his life at least, he had been something else entirely. How could I reconcile the sweet, gentle, slightly boring person I had known with this charged, accusing letter, these little bags of spells? What did it mean? How was it related to his death? What did my cousin Xavier have to do with it? Was Xavier the "evil" that the letter spoke of? Was I "the girl"? Or was this all some other fairy story that had nothing to do with me? I spilled out the contents of each bag and tried to make sense of it. But the seeds and stones, feathers, dust and spices meant nothing at all to me.

I thought about the box I had found buried in the roots of the apple tree. I had been so shocked by the memories that had come to me when I opened it, and then so devastated by what had come after, that I hadn't really thought about why I had remembered them in the first place, or what the box had done to evoke them. If I dug around the roots of other trees in the orchard where my uncle worked would I find other boxes, or little bags of spells? Would they evoke memories I had lost as well?

"Who were you?" I asked aloud, as if the officious little room of secrets would tell me anything about Uncle Oscar. I got no reply.

I gathered up the collection of papers and strange relics. I felt fear curl and clench in my midsection as I shoved the things in a knapsack I had brought for that purpose. The spirit bags, with their burden of mysteries, slithered to the bottom, while the papers crinkled on top. I felt both uneasy and frustrated. I was so tired of questions. How I wished someone would give me answers.

Outside of the bank, I thought I caught a glimpse of Xavier across the parking lot; leaning up against a pasture fence, snow making little stars glimmer in his back hair. At first, I felt a familiar flutter of pleasure at the sight of his face, and I started towards him. Then all of the terrible images I had seen a few nights before crowded into my mind and my steps faltered. I saw his expression lift at my approach and darken when I hesitated. We stood, eyes locked, only the snow falling between us. Then I heard the hiss of tires on wet asphalt and Colter's truck swished into my field of vision, effectively eclipsing any sight of Xavier. By the time Colter parked his truck next to the Holy Terror, Xavier had vanished, as if he had never been there at all.

19.

HOW NANAHUATZIN FOUND GRAIN

A story from Mexico

One day, the god Quetzalcoatl discovered corn and grain locked inside a great mountain.

Now Quetzalcoatl was a powerful god but even he could not collect this grain. He pounded with his serpent tail. He blazed with the heat of a dragon. He spoke words of power. None of it unlocked the mountain. Quetzalcoatl knew the seeds and grains would help the world. He knew if they were given to the earth they would germinate and feed his people. But the mountain stayed fast closed.

Finally Quetzalcoatl went to the god Nanahuatzin and asked that he send his lightning bolts to crack the mountain to pieces. Now, Nanahuatzin was the most humble of the gods, letting his light flash only rarely, and hiding himself the rest of the time. But Nanahuatzin loved the earth, and knew seeds would benefit the world. So he wielded his fire, stronger even than the mountain itself, and broke it open. The seeds spilled and the gods of rain and wind snatched them, so they could grow.

Without Nanahuatzin, we would have no corn. Quetzacoatl found it, but Nanahuatzin set it free.

20.

Colter leapt from his black truck. He had been trying to contact me for days, and I had been staving off his calls for many reasons, not the least of which was I felt embarrassed and confused by my behavior in the kitchen with him the night of my uncle's death. I am not the kind of person who runs around kissing men I hardly know. I am not the kind of person who runs around kissing men, period. That I was attracted to Colter went without saying. That I seemed incapable of controlling that attraction disturbed me a great deal.

And sure enough, my body again helplessly responded to Colter's unbridled virility, even in a parking lot, in a snowstorm, with my uncle's pathetic effects zipped up in a knapsack slung over my shoulder. Colter seemed impervious to the cold, his navy parka open, his blond hair flecked with snowflakes. He reached a hand out to pluck a lock of brown hair out of my face and I trembled, but not from the cold.

"Esmeralda. I've been so worried about you," he said.

"Thanks," I said.

"Can I buy you a cup of coffee?" he asked. "Hot chocolate? You look chilled."

I gazed into his blue eyes, soft with concern and found my mouth unhinging, heard myself saying, "Yes. Yes, all right." He smiled and held out his hand. I took it, suddenly grateful for its warmth. I didn't even glance at the fence where Xavier had been standing.

Colter led me to a nearby coffee house called Blue Cups. He ordered cinnamon cappuccinos. They arrived to our table, frothy and steamy, along with two chocolate croissants. Jubilant holiday shoppers carrying bags of gifts crowded at the tables and around the counter. Holly and mistletoe decorated the walls. A cheerful song about snowmen tinkled faintly in the background. I dimly remembered it was the Christmas season even as I felt the now familiar heaviness settle around my heart.

"Listen, Esme," said Colter. "I'm going to cut to the chase, because I know you're very busy." He leaned across the table. "I hardly know you. We've just met. And I know this is very presumptuous and not really any of my business. But I'm worried." The sincerity in his voice made my throat catch a little. "You're so young and you have such a big burden right now. I don't know how well your uncle provided for you, but even if he left you some money, I imagine you could use some help. Am I right?"

He was very right. Uncle Oscar had a little money set aside, but it was just enough to get him decently buried, not enough even to get Miguel and Ignacio and I through the next few months. My uncle had been a very successful farmer but not an astute businessman. Under his contract with Olstein, everything he grew ultimately belonged to the Olstein company. I was still sifting through his papers, but so far I hadn't found anything resembling the kind of fortune that would be needed to get Miguel and Ignacio through school, myself through college, all of us on our way to a bright future. Instead, our futures were as insubstantial and unpromising as the bubbles of foam in my cappuccino.

I didn't say any of this out loud to Colter. I didn't need to. He was a successful business owner, vintner and farmer; he probably knew more about my financial situation than I did. I just nodded my head and sipped my coffee.

"I have an offer for you," he said, taking a deep breath. "It's going to sound a little crazy, but just let me run through the whole scenario." He reached his hand out to mine. "It's like this, Esme. I'm a good businessman. But I'm not really creative. I know how to run things. I know how make money. I know how to make deals. That's what I do, and I'm good at it. But a guy like me needs creative people around him. People like you." He tugged on my fingers and they tingled lightly. "I'd like you to be the publicity manager for my new winery. You'd build my website and write press releases, content for brochures, stuff like that. Help with logos, marketing strategy. I know you could do a really good job with it. And I'd pay you a very fair salary. More than you could make anywhere else in Mattawa." He stroked each of my fingers as he talked, light, but emphatic touches. The tingling spread up my arm. "Your brothers are strong, experienced farm laborers. I would gladly give them summer jobs in the vineyards; let them work their way up the ladder. Hell, one of them might even want to learn the wine trade. I'll need apprentices once things really get off the ground here." He went on, still tantalizingly brushing my fingertips with his. My lips grew heavy, my heartbeat quickened. "I know you might not have envisioned this for yourself. I know your uncle meant for you to leave here after college. But I'd like to help you. I'd like you to stay. With me."

With a great effort, I pulled my hand out from under his. "Why?" I asked. I clasped my hands under the table, daring him to try seducing me again. "I'm not the only creative person in this area, surely."

He ducked his head. "All right," he said. "Cards on the table. I find you… I don't even know how to say this. I find you…" His blue eyes suddenly pinned my own. "I find you breathtakingly beautiful. I find you incredibly sexy. Believe me when I tell you Esme, I could scour the country right now and I wouldn't find another woman like you. You are very, very rare and I want you." He cleared his throat and set his teeth. "I want to get to know you. I want to keep you close to me, for a hundred reasons I can't explain." His voice had an edge to it that made my heart pound. "This is not the time to be romancing you. I get that." He leaned forward. "But I can help you. I have enormous resources. You have no idea, really, about what I can do. I'm offering you help and in return..."

"Yes?"

"In return... you stay and work with me. And see what happens. What do you say?"

My mind flipped to the scene in my uncle's kitchen, just a few days ago, the passion I felt, the way Colter's hands and mouth had kindled it. With the memory came a familiar, helpless, sexual ache, one that seemed to arise every time I was in a certain proximity to him. "I don't know..."

"I can help you," he urged. "Please."

I could swear his voice sent little ghost fingers caressing my skin. He was so devastatingly attractive. In the coffee house, women of all ages were turning to look at him, and at me. I felt helpless, repelled and aroused, all at once.

I said, only half joking, "You really are something, Justin Colter." I felt a twinge of doubt and misery even as I said those words, but I brushed it aside as Colter leaned forward and I caught a whiff of his tantalizing scent, warm and musky, mixing with the cinnamon smell of the coffee.

"I want you to feel safe. I'll draw up an ironclad contract, if you like. A fair wage for work fairly done. But—" here his mouth lifted slightly "—I'd be a liar, Esme, if I didn't say I wanted something... more." The "more" in his words was a palpable energy between us, and I felt it, like a flare of heat in the middle of the table.

My lips felt heavy as I parted them to say, "Can I think about it?"

He brought his fist lightly down on the table. "Of course," he said after a moment. "But don't think too much or too long. It's a solid offer."

"Thank you," I said, and meant it. It was a solid offer. I would be a fool not to take it. And I didn't fully understand why I wasn't grabbing it on the spot.

❄

From The Mattawa Weekly News, December 14, 2012
In "News From Appletown" by Esmeralda Ulloa

This week, I will be honoring the story of Santa Claus, also known as Father Christmas and St. Nicholas.

The original St Nicholas was the bishop of Myra, in Turkey in the 4th century. He is famous for giving gifts to the poor, and for being the patron saint of children and sailors. His official feast day was December 6, and it is for this reason that he probably has been forever associated with Christmas.

The modern conception of Santa Claus blends Norse, Dutch and German mythology with the original saint, giving rise to the current story of a jolly elf who lives in the North Pole and brings gifts to good children on Christmas Eve.

Below are original Letters to Santa Claus from Janie Gray's second grade classroom at Wahluke Elementary School. Along with Janie Gray and her second graders, I wish you the best of the season and a very merry Christmas.

"Dear Santa,

Please give me a Nintendo and Legos for Christmas, my dad would like a tractor and my mom a duck. You can forget my little brother he was bad yesterday. Love from, Carlos"

"Dear Santa,

I hope you have a Merry Christmas. Do you ever get presents for the reindeer? I think Rudolph would like a toy, too. Sincerely yours, Tina"

"Dear Santa,

Please tell the baby Jesus to be good to my grandpa Paco in heaven. I think he might be lonely without us. Merry Christmas and thank you, Alfonso Fernandez"

21.

In my dream, I saw Xavier at the pasture fence by the bank parking lot again. As before, it was snowing, and flakes of glimmered in his raven wing hair. I approached him, feeling safe this time, because Fitzsimmons padded by my side. The big dog walked imperturbably across the asphalt, his white tail waving like a flag.

Mattawa is a town in the middle of nowhere. The school borders a wilderness. The grocery store backs up against a vineyard. The bank parking lot is right next to a pasture. In the winter it is a perfect white expanse, broken only by rabbit paths and the occasional black fence post. Xavier stood in front of the barbed wire. He must have been standing there for some time, as his clothes were lightly dusted with snow.

I watched Fitz greet Xavier with real affection. My cousin knelt and stroked him, speaking in a soft voice. I said sharply, "Are you putting him under a spell?"

Xavier rose and regarded me out of cool gray eyes. "I have no talent with animals, Esme. He just knows an enemy from a friend." His hand left off patting Fitz as his gaze narrowed. "What stories have you been told about me, Esme?"

"No stories," I said. "I found a box buried in the orchard. And I remembered what I forgot."

"Who left the box?"

"Uncle Oscar, I think."

"Really? I doubt you remember anything then."

"I think I remember enough," I said hotly. "Tell me, Xavier. Did you kill my Uncle Oscar?"

His black eyebrows swooped together. "Why would I do that, Esmeralda?"

"Because…" I said, and faltered. I looked down at Fitzsimmons, who was looking up at me, his head cocked to one side. "Because you're evil," I said lamely. "Because he sent you away." The words felt heavy and strange on my tongue but I kept talking. "You are a magician and you burned him because…"

"Yes, because…?" he prompted, his head was cocked to one side too, in a mocking echo of Fitzsimmons.

"Because you want me for your own," I finished lamely.

The big dog opened his mouth, almost like a smile, his tongue hanging out of his mouth. He looked adorable and clownish. He seemed to be saying, "That's a good one, Esme. Tell me another." I heard Xavier laugh and suddenly I was tempted to join them. The whole thing sounded so ridiculous, once I said it out loud. I shook my head. What else had I remembered? It all seemed very far away. "Oh, Xavier," I said. "Who are you? Please, just tell me, who the hell are you?"

He leaned towards me. He pursed his lips and blew his breath on my face. I felt pierced by the sudden warmth. I had not realized how cold I was, out in the parking lot, with snow wetting my hair. Xavier's breath touched me in my very center, and I felt delightful little flames licking around my heart, teasing it to life. "I am the one who wants you free, preciosa," he whispered.

I breathed in warmth. "Tell me, who I am."

He shook his head. "Wake up, preciosa," he said, his voice tinged with desperation. "Wake up."

I woke in Annie's the bunkhouse. Blob and Fitzsimmons slept by the stove, dog-snoring in concert. The fire had burned out in the night. It was very cold. My brothers slept in their bunks nearby, smaller brother-snores joining the concert the two dogs had begun. It was early in the morning, and the day of my uncle's memorial service. I could hear Annie outside, feeding her chickens, clucking at them while they clucked back.

I rolled over and sat up. The dream about Xavier lingered, like a whiff of perfume, faint but sweet. What did it mean? I looked at Fitz's sleeping form by the fire. In my dream, Fitz had liked Xavier, welcomed his touch. *He knows a friend from an enemy.*

"It's a dream," I told myself. "And none of it matters today, anyway. This morning, it's about Uncle Oscar." I hauled on my boots and headed out into the cold, snow covered world, to get ready to say goodbye to him forever.

Desert Aire is a very fancy retirement community just outside of Mattawa. It has a golf course, a clubhouse and a meeting hall that is used fairly often for community events. Annie had helped me rent it for my uncle's memorial service. She had ordered flowers and arranged for speakers and singers. She had been a wonderful friend. I knew that my brothers and I could not indefinitely live in her bunkhouse, like kids on a sleepover. But it had been a solid comfort for all of us, to be in her home, to be together. I thought about Colter's offer and how easy—and complicated—my life would become if I took it. He was offering more than a high paying job and security for my brothers. Did I want to take that offer? Part of me did, very much. But part of me held back. Something about it didn't feel right, although it all seemed so perfect on the surface.

I put on a black dress and tights. I combed my long, brown hair and tied it back in a barrette to keep it neat. I brushed my lashes with mascara. By then, my brothers were awake and stirring. Annie clanged in the house, brisk and determined. She greeted everyone with a kiss, gold glasses flashing on her sharp face. Fluff, fat and heavy with a brood of puppies soon to be born, also greeted everyone with a kiss, slobbery and loving. And I, as I had so many times before in the past few days, sank into a numb, dull space, where everything seemed to happen from a very long distance. It was like curling up into a cocoon, or burying myself like a seed in the earth for a long, dull, dreamless sleep.

❄

I remained only dimly aware of the memorial service transpiring. Many, many people from the town were there, from all walks. Alex Sanchez, the police chief, with his bristling crew cut and mustache, friends of Miguel and Ignacio, sober and subdued in their best clothes, Dane Olstein and his wife, along with employees of the orchard, apple tree hobbyists from farms and universities all over the country..

I had written a speech and I fought to keep my voice steady as I spoke in front of everyone. I talked about Uncle Oscar's kindness and generosity. I concluded by saying, "Uncle Oscar always said the most honorable work in the world was making food for people. 'Food is life,' he said. 'Good food makes for good life.' Today, we honor a very good life indeed."

Later, I stood in a receiving line and greeted all the people who came. I did this mechanically, even when Justin Colter's big hands engulfed my own, and his blue eyes blazed down at me. I simply nodded and turned to the next person. I could tell he felt cheated and bereft, but I didn't care.

It was a pair of big, brown eyes that suddenly lifted me out of my stupor. Veronica Fernandez stood in front of me, holding out her slender hand. I gripped it, harder than I'd meant to, and a silver ring she wore on her finger cut into my flesh. I was vividly reminded of a scene in her grandfather's house, so sadly similar to this.

"Veronica," I said.

"I'm so sorry, Miss," she murmured. "This is such a bad time for us both."

She tried to take her hand from mine, but I gripped it even harder. She looked around, confused and self- conscious. I maneuvered out of the receiving line, aware of my brothers' attention, but too intent on my thoughts and feelings to pay it any mind. "Veronica," I said, trying to control the urgency in my voice, feeling like I was swimming up from the bottom of a very deep well. "There was—there was—a woman at your house, the day your grandfather was found. You were talking to her as I was leaving."

"Yes," Veronica said. "That is Tia Donna."

"Your Aunt… Donna?" My heart skipped a beat. "Her name is Donna—Donna of the Saints?"

Veronica nodded. "Donna del Santos." She still seemed confused and a little afraid that I had left the receiving line to speak to her. I could see many people in the room, craning their necks to look at us. Justin Colter, who had been lingering by the door, had started over in our direction.

Quickly I said, "She told me I needed to contact her. That you would know where to find her and I should ask you."

Puzzled, Veronica said, "Yes. It is quite some ways from here, across the river. But I can tell you how to get there."

"Will you write the address down and give it to Annie Mortmain?"

"The newspaper lady?" Everyone in town knew Annie.

"Please. Before you leave. It's very important. And," I glanced at Colter, suddenly afraid he could hear us and not wanting him to, although I couldn't say why. "And… don't let anyone else see you do it."

"Yes, of course, Miss," said Veronica. Her brown eyes widened as

Justin Colter sidled up and grasped my elbow.

"Is everything all right, Esme?" he asked me.

I nodded at Veronica, who backed away, eyes both admiring and a little fearful as I turned to Colter and tried to shrug lightly, although my insides were vibrating like a plucked string.

"Oh, yes," I said to him, keeping my voice steady. "Veronica is just a girl I hadn't seen in awhile, that's all. We know... some of the same people." I gave him a quick, dismissive smile and took my place in the receiving line again.

Colter watched me for a while, a slight frown creasing his features. It was fine if he kept his eyes on me, even if it was a little disconcerting. Because I don't think he noticed pretty Veronica Fernandez, borrowing a pen from Annie and writing something in one of her notebooks before taking her leave. I didn't know why I felt relieved about that, but I did.

22.

Tia Donna lived across the Columbia River, in a little town called Vantage. It was a thirty-minute drive from Mattawa. Annie didn't ask why I had to go there like a bat out of hell, directly after the memorial service. She just jutted her sharp chin at the Holy Terror and told me to come home before dark. My brothers looked wistful and a little bereft as I kissed them and told them I would be home soon. I could see Miguel forming a protest, or getting ready to ask if he could come to Vantage with me. I wasn't sure how I could head him off, but just then Colter swooped in and offered to run the boys back to Annie's farm in his truck. Miguel and Ignacio never turned down an opportunity to ride around in Colter's giant black machine. I will never know the attraction boys have for big trucks but I was grateful for the distraction and flashed Colter a smile, as I jumped in the Holy Terror, still wearing my dress and black tights. He watched me blat out of Desert Aire, spraying gravel and exhaust in my wake, his good looks marred by the tight frown on his face.

The highway out of Mattawa runs along the Columbia River gorge, a beautiful swath of silvery water surrounded by high, red cliffs. Snow covered mountains rose up on the other side of the river. A flock of geese arrowed across the sky.

As I put distance between myself and Mattawa, I felt my head clearing. It was like a wind cutting in on off the water and blowing debris away. How in the world had I forgotten about my conversation with the mysterious woman, who had promised answers to my many questions? With each mile and each breath I felt a little stronger and a little more aware. The dull, sick feelings of the past few days retreated. By the time I crossed the river, I felt positively sharp, and more alive than I had felt in days and days. *If only I had found a way to come here sooner*, I thought to myself.

"I've been lost in dreams," I murmured, as I rolled off the highway and into the little town of Vantage, with a main street even smaller and shorter than Mattawa's.

Tia Donna's house was a tiny cottage at the end of a long, winding driveway. Built on a cliff, it overlooked the river and the hills across it. I pulled in and shut off the Holy Terror's engine. I hoped she would be home. I wasn't sure what I would do if she was not.

Feeling more than a little intimidated and nervous, I slid from the van and walked to the door. I took a moment to collect my thoughts. Would she remember me? How would I approach her? What would I say first?

But the door opened before I could raise my fist to knock on it, and everything that had been in my head was wiped away because it was Xavier who answered. His gray-gold eyes blazed. He held out his arms to me. I smelled cedar and smoke. Warmth kindled my heart.

"Precisoa," he said. "It has taken you forever to come to me."

I jumped into his arms and his warm lips met mine, and just like that, I woke up. I felt dazzled and clear all at once, as I drew back and knew him for exactly who he was. "You were never evil," I said, knowing it was true.

He smiled while his scarred thumb brushed my cheek. "I was a regular kid, Esme. Some might have called me a devil."

"You're not my cousin," I added.

His smile widened and he shook his head. "Not exactly."

"It depends on how you look at it." Tia Donna's husky voice floated from the inside of the house. "You and Xavier share a similar power, so you might call each other 'cousin.' But you are not blood related. Someone's been telling you a pack of half truths to keep you confused and afraid."

I peered over Xavier's shoulder and saw her, tiny and brown, her arms crossed over her chest. The room reminded me of Annie's house, with its splashes of color, rugs, paintings and thrift store furniture. Tia Donna wore the same vivid green skirt, and a beautifully embroidered blouse. A flowered shawl covered her sharp shoulders. "Come in the house," she said, flashing her little teeth and beckoning.

"Tia Donna," I whispered, as Xavier took my hand and led me across the threshold. "How could I have forgotten you?"

"Well," she said, welcoming me into her tough embrace. "Your uncle made sure you forgot almost everything." She gestured to a polished wood table and bench. "Come," she said. "Sit down. We haven't much time, but you need a to gather your strength for what is to come."

I slid onto the bench, feeling a little weak in the knees. A big window looked out onto the coiling river and red cliffs. A pot of spicy tea steamed on the table. Xavier eased beside me. I reached over to tangle my fingers with his. Tia Donna sat across from me and I looked at her face—it reminded me of a dried apple, wrinkled, brown and sweet.

"My uncle… made me forget you?"

Tia Donna nodded. "Your uncle Oscar was an encantador, Esmeralda. Un mago," she said. "And a very good one in his day. He's made you forget quite a bit, including who you are."

"Uncle Oscar was a—wizard?"

"Of sorts." Tia Donna inclined her head as she poured the tea. "As am I. Both of us very minor magic workers, I assure you. But yes, we both studied el arte de magia blanca. White magic. For me, it is healing arts, women's magic. For him, it had to do with the harvest, planting, and such. It is so with many people. Some call it intuition, yes? A certain sensitivity? But these sensitivities can be explored, and strengthened. And this is el arte de magia."

I nodded. I thought of Uncle Oscar's boxes, the little bags of spells I found at the bank, my locks of hair so safely secreted. On the one hand, it was ridiculous—how could my uncle be a magician? But on the other hand, it made sense, in a way that no other explanation for the boxes or the spirit bags had.

"Your uncle might have gone along very quietly, as I do, letting people come to him for help, working very small magics in small ways, with growing things. But then he found you, Esmeralda, in an orphanage in Arizona, and he became very ambitious indeed."

"Me?" I sipped spicy tea as Xavier shifted on the bench beside me.

"You are one of Xilonen's daughters," she said. "A child of la tierra. You have a great power. You can put your hands in the earth and call the seeds to grow. You can touch the trees and make them bear fruit. Your Uncle Oscar recognized what you were and he took you."

"Xilonen?"

"She has many names, in many countries, but that is the name I know her by. The Goddess of Corn. That is what she is called in Mexico."

"And I am her… daughter," I said doubtfully.

"She has marked you, yes. So you have the power to move the earth, and to make the plants grow. Roses in snow. Apples in midwinter. Flowers from the sand. A little seed, your breath, your hands. You are born to serve the people, by her grace."

"But I don't… I don't…" I faltered.

"Your uncle made you forget," said Xavier softly.

"But…. Why?"

Tia Donna sighed. "He told himself the lies that all men tell themselves when they are capturing and then exploiting a woman of power. First he said, 'I will give her a home, and in return she will help me make a name for myself as a cultivator of the earth.' So he generously adopted not only you, but also your brothers and he took your family intact to Washington. And indeed he began to make a name for himself as a cultivator of the earth, using his gifts, but mostly your powers. He said, 'When she is fourteen years-old, I will free her from service.' He wanted just enough time to get the apples going. Seven years."

"But then…"

"He still thought he needed more time, of course. He tells himself he's a Mexican national, an immigrant, underpaid; it can be hard for him to get a piece of land of his own. So. He works his way up to orchard manager for Olstein. But still he is not satisfied. It is always like that, with fame and success and material goods. Each thing leads to something more. A man says: I will stop working when I get to 'this,' and then 'this' arrives and still it is not want he wants. And I told Oscar, I said to him—"

"You told him that his pride would invoke an evil—" I said.

"Yes, yes," said Tia Donna. She brought down her tiny, brown fist on the table. "The more he used you, the more… aware other powers in this world—and out of this world—would become of your potential. A child of Xilonen is not meant to serve anyone but whom she chooses. But your uncle, he kept wanting more. Just a little more. And so, when your fourteenth birthday came—"

"On midwinter—" I looked at Xavier.

"He arranged to steal your gifts again, and told himself he was not stealing them. 'I will send her to college,' he said that time. 'I will make sure she has a good start in life.' But it was all lies."

I grasped Xavier's fingers tightly. "Why did he send you away?"

Tia Donna's gaze slid to Xavier and she smiled, showing her little, white teeth. "Well. It is rare to have a daughter of the goddess born. It is rarer still to have two children with ancient powers in the same community. But it was so. Xavier is a child of Nanahuatzin, the sweet god of lightning, sun and sacrifice. And because he is my grandchild, I allowed him to be free to choose his destiny as he saw fit. And all he ever wanted and all he ever loved, from the time he was a little boy… was you, Esmeralda."

I felt warmth flow in my chest and I twined my fingers more tightly with Xavier's hot ones. "On your fourteenth birthday, I was going to tell you all about us," he said. "I was going to ask you—" his voice became choked and shook his head. "Never mind what I was going to ask you. It doesn't matter. Your uncle never even gave me the chance. Before the year turned he had seen to it that you were his, and then he took those cursed wooden boxes and wove such spells that just breathing the air in the orchards drove me mad and made you forget me. But he couldn't take everything." Tears glimmered on his long eyelashes. "Not everything. He could steal your waking life. He could steal your power. But he couldn't take your dreams. And I told Abuela Donna—"

"Eighteen years-old he was, and hot as a coal; steam coming off his skin." Tia Donna's pearly little teeth flashed.

"I said to her, 'I will save Esmeralda. I will steal her back from her uncle'—"

"But it doesn't work that way," said Tia Donna. "Seven years you were yoked again." Her bright gaze flicked to Xavier. "It is just as well. You couldn't have married the girl when she was fourteen, anyway."

He muttered something and turned his head away. I felt a laugh building in my chest, because I knew what he was thinking. I would have married him at fourteen. I would have run off with him without a second's hesitation. I would have done anything he asked.

"Uncle must have been quite a powerful magic worker," I whispered. "To make me forget you." I looked at the tears on Xavier's lashes and the laugh in my chest abruptly became something else.

Tia Donna snorted and got up from the table, to the other room. I watched her walk away, her green skirt swishing, and then let my gaze drift back to Xavier. There were so many things I wanted to say to him, but they hovered in my tight chest like birds in a cage. Instead, I let my fingers tug on the worn leather band he wore on his wrist. He looked down on it, and at me, and the sadness in his gray eyes pierced my heart.

Tia Donna returned, her little feet clacking on the floor. She dropped an object in front of me and said. "There. I kept it safe, as I said, just in case your Uncle balked again. It was the least I could do for my Xavier, while he was kept from his heart's desire."

I stared down at the little carved, wooden box she had put before me and felt my skin prickle. "I've already found one of these, buried in the orchard by my uncle's house."

Her gray brows arched as she sat across from me again. "What did it contain?"

"Dirt," I said. "And… memories, I guess." I shuddered, thinking of how they had engulfed me the moment I opened it. "Bad things, most of which I wish I didn't know."

She nodded. "Your uncle made sure that if either Xavier or I tried to interfere with you, the magic would drive you, or us away. Such boxes litter his orchards. All of them contain spells he made, of one kind or another. Was this box you found full of memories about your uncle? Or your early life in Arizona? Stories of the goddess Xilonen?"

"I remembered things about Xavier," I said, in a small, cold voice.

Xavier made a sound and shifted in his seat. Tina Donna grimaced and gestured with her chin at the box on the table. "I see," she said. "Well. Open this one, then."

I tried to keep my hands from shaking as I fumbled with lid. Unlike the one in the orchard, this box was clean and well polished, the carvings of fruits and flowers very clear, intricate and beautiful. I unconsciously clenched my teeth as I pulled up the lid, but I didn't need to. There was no assault of bad memories in this box. Instead, I smelled a heavenly fragrance, like cedar and cinnamon and apple blossoms and rain. And instead of a tidal wave of terrible feelings, I felt a gentle opening in my mind, like a blossom unfurling its petals in the sun.

23.

Uncle had been strange all the week before Christmas. He spent long hours in his shed, and was often away at night, leaving me to babysit my little brothers, which was HORRIBLE, because they never did ANYTHING I said and I HATED them for it. "Go to bed!" I would tell them and they would laugh and stick out their tongues and lock me out of their room. "Clean the dishes!" I would say, and they would walk away and leave the crusted dishes in the sink, where they smelled bad. Then Uncle would yell like it was my fault, when it was really his.

But a part of me didn't even care about any of that, because Xavier had invited me to the Midwinter Bonfires and Uncle was letting me go with him. The week before, I had driven all the way to the Tri-Cities with my friend Diana and her mother to get Christmas presents for my stupid brothers, but also to buy the most beautiful dress I could afford with the money I'd saved from picking fruit. I had also gotten my hair done, and my nails painted and almost fifty dollars worth of make up from Merle Norman because I was going to look amazing for Xavier, and he was going to be struck dumb by my beauty and the whole night was going to be amazing. I had bought Xavier a present too, after much agonizing and talking late into the night with Diana, (who was completely jealous that I even had a boyfriend, much less one who was older, and totally nice and handsome as a dream). I had bought a really, really cool leather wristband, with a silver buckle, and I knew it would look beautiful on Xavier's perfect, brown wrist. Sometimes I loved Xavier so much, I hurt with it. I would be walking through the halls at Wahluke High and I would think of him and my chest would get tight and my knees would go loose, and I would have to lean up against wall until the throbbing in my heart subsided...

The memories that washed into my brain were so very different from the ones I had experienced in my kitchen a few days before. Not all of them were pleasant, and many of them weren't even very interesting, but they were detailed, and specific and real. I had the sensation of thousands of puzzle pieces locking into place in my head, and of all of them building a picture that was whole and complete.

Uncle Oscar had called me away from dancing that night and he had looked so lonely, I had gone with him, even though Xavier seemed angry about it. Uncle said he had a present for my birthday and I needed to look at it now, right now. Why should Xavier be angry? It might be a very nice present. It might be my own horse! Or a check for a thousand dollars! Or a trip to New York City! But instead of a nice present, Uncle Oscar took me into his work shed and cut off a lock of my hair. Then he showed me a little wooden box, and he said, "Open this," and I did, and I suddenly felt so sleepy. He said, "Put your fingers in this earth for me, and dig, Esme," and I did, even though I was wearing a nice dress...

"He took my—he took my gifts! He took my power! He took my life." The words sounded like they were spoken by someone else; they sounded torn from my throat. "I-I," I held my hands up in front of my face, marveling, because I'd never really seen them before, not really. "I could have—I could have—I could have—hurt—him—but I didn't because I-I loved him—and I let him—I-I let him put me to sleep—but why did he—why did he—" The raw, awfulness of my voice broke into something that sounded like wailing and screaming, and it was terrible, but it was also all right. I thought I might choke on my own screams, but at the same time I had the sense of some huge block inside my chest being moved by my tears, being washed away, like a clot of dead leaves and sticks being swept down a river. I felt wonderful, even though it hurt.

I was only vaguely aware of Tia Donna's footsteps retreating, and of Xavier's warm arms holding me, his hands stroking my hair, his voice murmuring. I don't know how long I cried, but when I was done, I felt as clear and empty and fresh as a green glade in springtime.

"He trapped my soul like a butterfly in a net," I whispered. "And then he pinned me down, numbed my brains and robbed me of my strength." I looked at my hands. "The power leaks out like gold from my fingers. I saw it happen while I fell asleep. Twice."

I heard Tia Donna clear her throat behind me. "If you were alive in Aztec times, in Mexico, the magicians would have skinned you and thrown you in the fire to take your power," she rasped. "In Hawaii, they would have put you in a live volcano. In ancient Europe they would have made you a queen and killed your husband. You are lucky your uncle only poured your power into tubs of earth and then locked your memories in a box, child."

"I don't feel lucky," I said putting my face in my hands. "I forgot… my soul, my heart. I forgot everything."

Xavier said gently, "All this time, you have been trying to remember who you are."

I looked up at him. "All those fairy tales. Mexican folklore. All those dreams of you."

"The stories were a map you tried to draw for yourself. And the dreams were my way of trying to keep us together."

"But…. What was the other box? The one I found the night Uncle Oscar disappeared? Those memories were distorted. Real and not real." I shook my head.

"I think he prepared the box in case I tried to stop him that night," Xavier said. "He said he would make you hate me, if I tried to release you, or Tia Donna interfered."

"Why did he try to dig it up in the orchard last week?"

Tia Donna gave me a sharp look. "How do you know he did?" she asked.

"Because it was by a pile of apples, in a hole…" I trailed off, thinking of the neat little pile of the very best of Uncle Oscar's crop, Burford Reds, Arkansas Blacks, Ashmead Kernals, bright skins gleaming against the plain brown earth. They were conveniently located next to a spade and a half dug hole, the exact same apples I had collected for—

"Justin Colter," I groaned. "Justin Colter fixed it so I'd find that box. Because, because—" I looked at Xavier. "He wanted me not to trust you, because—" I almost choked, feeling sick to my stomach. "He doesn't want me to know who you are. He doesn't want you to come near me," I whispered. "…What does he want from me?"

Xavier's arms tightened. I heard Tia Donna's heels click as she crossed into my field of vision. "He wants your power child."

"My power?"

"His kind always want more power."

"He's the skinwalker," I said, feeling my stomach crawling up in to my throat.

Tia Donna nodded grimly. "My brother Paco recognized him. He was working for the construction company Colter had engaged to build his winery. He immediately knew the creature for what it was. One gets sensitive to such things when one's sister is a mage, yes?"

"You were there, too," I said to Xavier.

"I hoped I'd see you, of course," he said.

"Paco recognized Colter for what he was and he tried to warn me that a demon had come to Mattawa. But Colter caught up to him before Xavier or I could help." She shook her head sadly. "Although what could we really do? Your Uncle fixed it so we had such a terrible time even entering town."

"Colter killed your brother?"

She nodded.

"And he killed Uncle Oscar, too?"

She nodded.

I thought swiftly. "Uncle Oscar wanted to warn me, I think." I looked at Xavier, feeling my heartbeat quicken. "I showed him your picture, and he pretended not to know you. We were with Colter at the time. He must have been trying to protect you. He knew you would help me get away. And then he went looking for this," I pointed to the wooden box. "The little box of memories he had stolen from me. He tore the house apart looking for it. He wanted me to remember you, I think, in the end. But I didn't reach him in time to tell him what you told me, Tia… that you had it, all along." My voice cracked. "Colter must have killed Uncle Oscar because he knew Uncle Oscar would try to set me free…"

"If he even meant to set you free," Xavier muttered. "Maybe he would have kept you for another seven years."

"Oh, I'm sure he wouldn't," I said.

Tia Donna said, "Don't judge too harshly, Xavier."

"I'll judge as harshly as I like. He made her forget me for seven years and he might as well have torn my heart to pieces."

"What I don't understand," I said, "is if Colter's so powerful, how come he doesn't just kill me outright, the way he did Paco and Uncle Oscar?"

"Because he doesn't want to kill you, Esme. He killed those men because they got in his way. No. He wants your power. And for that, he needs you alive and he needs your permission," Tia Donna said.

My chin dropped. "What?"

"No one can have your power unless you give it. You are a child of the goddess, Esmeralda."

"But you just said my uncle took my power—"

"Yes. But he always asked first."

"He asked a child," Xavier muttered. "Of course she said yes."

"He might have put it like this: 'Do you mind sitting here?' 'Would you put your hands here?' 'May I take a lock of your pretty hair?' 'Why don't you forget about everything?'"

I nodded at Tia Donna, remembering. *He had asked, of course. He had asked both times. But why would I refuse him? He was my uncle and I trusted him.*

"But the children of the gods always have a choice, Esmeralda," Tia Donna went on. "You could have said 'no.' But you probably didn't know how to. We so seldom teach our girl children to say, 'no.'"

I thought about Colter, and all the conversations we'd had since he came to town, and all of the bargains he had tried to make. "So far, I've managed not to say 'yes' to Colter"

"Well, he has yet to make the offer you absolutely can't refuse," Xavier said. "But he will. And very soon."

"Well, you'll save me, right?"

He shook his head while Tia Donna laughed, her little teeth gleaming. "What? What's so funny?" I said, looking from one to the other. "Don't I get a hero? Isn't that why you wanted me to find you, Tia Donna?"

"Of course you get a hero," Xavier said. "But you are your own hero, Esme."

"I..." I trailed off, looking from Tia Donna to Xavier in disbelief. "I have to fight Colter?"

"It must come down to you. It is you he wants."

"But... but I don't even know who I am!" I wailed. I turned to Xavier. "You've had seven years—more!—to-to-to wield your powers! Learn your craft! You could make your hands light a fire when you were seventeen! You must be able to throw a bolt of lightning on him—or you." I turned to Tia Donna. "Make a spirit bag—"

"We can do a great deal," Xavier said. "But we can't speak for you, Esmeralda! Only you can—"

"But I am—I—" I stood up from the table. I felt my body go suddenly cold. "Why didn't you help me before?"

"I told you. Your Uncle Oscar sent me away. I couldn't have talked to you, or touched you—"

"But..." I turned to Tia Donna. "For that to happen... Didn't Xavier have to give his permission too?" I turned back to Xavier. "If you are like me... Didn't you have to choose to leave me? It's the same for you, isn't it? You have to give your permission in order for someone to take something away from you?"

Xavier's jaw clenched. He said through gritted teeth, "Yes. But if I did not go, your uncle said he would make it so you were afraid of me, so that you would hate the sight of me. The choice was mine, yes. But I couldn't bear the thought of your hatred. It was seven years without you, or having you run from me in fear."

"But.... How do you know I would have?"

His voice rose. "Esme, you already opened that other box of his. You went right under the spell he wove. You believed I was evil—"

"For a time! Yes! It worked. It did. But maybe you could have stayed and helped me fight it, Xavier. Like you are now." He looked at me, his face stricken. "You might have been able to help me remember sooner, if you'd stayed."

"I had to go, Esme." His voice was tight.

"That's a lie." I might as well have slapped him. He turned his face away from me with a hiss of pain.

"You wasted time too," Tia Donna said quietly. "Don't blame your lot on Xavier. Look to yourself, child." She said, "These are the facts. Your uncle bound you to him for seven years. That's a time of service no magician can break. Not me, not Xavier, and not even that bastard Colter. But Colter has been getting ready for you, Esme. He has been laying his traps, leading up to this night. He has orchestrated every second of it. He's frightened you and distracted you and made you helpless. And you have wasted time. Time when you could have been learning. Time when you could have been formulating a plan. So. Now we are here. In just a few short hours, at midnight, midwinter's day will begin. The season will change, you will turn twenty-one, and he will have his answer. Are you going to fight or not?"

All my anger dissolved as I was swept with cold fear. I swallowed. "Are my brothers… like me?" I looked at Tia Donna. "Can they help?"

She shook her head. "The goddess chose only you, Esme, just as only Xavier was the only one chosen from our family. From what I know, your brothers are delightful young men, and… utterly normal, I'm afraid."

I sighed. It had gotten dark outside in the time we had been talking. How long had I been sitting at the table with Xavier and Tia Donna? I fumbled in my pocket to look at my phone to check the time. I saw I had received a text message from Annie. "I must be so late getting home," I murmured, pushing a button to read the text.

My blood turned to ice in my veins. "Oh, God, no."

"Esme?"

"Annie says… the boys haven't come home. She asked… if I asked C-Colter to take them somewhere." I looked at Xavier. "Colter was supposed to take my brothers home from the memorial service. That was hours ago. Xavier. Colter has my little brothers."

❄

THE CREATION OF THE WORLD
From Aztec Mythology

All the gods had gathered together. For though the world had been made, time and history had not begun, for the beginning could only be made through an ending, and so a god had to be sacrificed. They built a bonfire, and looked at one another, to see which of the gods would be the next sun. Everyone looked to Tecciztecatl, handsome and strong, for he was the obvious hero. But Tecciztecatl hesitated, afraid to jump into the fire. He feared the pain, and he feared the sacrifice, and he feared the unknown. So he stood there, paralyzed, until finally, Nanahuatzin, least of the gods, took the plunge instead. So the world was made, not by the greatest, but by the least. Nanahuatzin became the sun, strong and warm, and the power from which all life would grow. And Tecciztecatl, shamed by his cowardice, followed him into the fire. But he only became the moon, with no light of his own, except what Nanahuatzin gave to him.

24.

"I let them go," I muttered. "Why? I didn't trust him." I shook my head. "But he said, 'I'll take the boys home,' and I wanted to come here so I…"

Tia Donna said, "Did you think dealing with a devil would be easy? He is wily and powerful. He makes people stupid—with lust, with envy, with anger, with pride. So you have been stupid. Welcome to the world, Esme. But you get another chance to be smart. Xavier does, too. Come. There is no time to be lost."

She flew around the room like a quick, brown and green bird, tossing twigs, feathers, little stones in a tiny cloth bag, making a charm for me to wear around my neck. Xavier grimly set about filling his pockets with an assortment of silver tokens and tools. He had not said a thing to me after I had voiced my accusation. The anger and blame I felt lay between us like a wall of stone.

My eye fell by the leather wristband he had worn for seven years. I had given it to him the night of the dance, fastened it on his arm with my heart pounding and my love for him a flower of flame in my mouth. I reached out. He froze, arm rigid, lips tight. I touched the wristband gently. “Xavier,” I said, my throat thick. “All this time…”

“Who cares?” He tried to brush me aside, but I held on tight.

“No,” I said. “I might not get a chance to say this and I want you to know… I loved you so much, and a part of me never stopped loving you. You were my everything, Xavier. I would have…” I choked. “I promise you, I would have, if he hadn’t. How can you forgive me for what I did? For saying ‘yes,’ to him, when I could have said ‘no’?”

Xavier’s voice wobbled. “It is I who needs to be forgiven. I couldn’t face the idea of you fearing me. But you were right. I should have stayed. I should have tried. Who knows what might have happened, if I’d had more faith?”

I swallowed. “Can we just say that we were kids?”

His stormy eyes searched mine. “No. I don’t know that we can,” he said. “Any time evil comes into a place it is because someone gives it permission. You were a child and did not really know what was happening. But I did, Esme. And—it is true—I have cursed myself for my weakness a hundred times. Can you forgive me? That you have to do this now all alone?”

“That I have to fight for myself? Oh, Xavier,” I breathed. “There is nothing to forgive.”

His kiss was like a promise, that time, sure and swift and hard. And I was whole when I kissed him back, for the first time in seven years.

❄

It is a very strange feeling to know that you are about to embark on an epic, magical battle with an ancient demon and you still have to climb into something like the Holy Terror to get across the Columbia River to find him. As the engine blatted to life, and the wind whistled through the bullet holes, I had to shake my head and laugh a little at the absurdity.

My cell phone didn’t seem to be working. Tia Donna said it

probably wouldn't from now on. "Modern conveniences balk in the vibrations of the ancient powers awakened," she said.

But Tia Donna had faith that I would have no trouble crossing the river to Colter, even in the Holy Terror. After all, he wanted me with him in Mattawa tonight. He wanted to capture my power before my twenty-first birthday.

Xavier and Tia Donna would have no such ease in crossing the river, however. "He's been keeping me out for days," Xavier said. "Why should tonight be any different?"

So we decided that I would go to Colter alone. Xavier would try to get to Annie's to fetch Fitzsimmons and Blob. "Colter hates those dogs," I pointed out. "And Annie thinks Fitz has special powers."

❄

Driving alone across the bridge to Mattawa, I felt strangely good. I realized for perhaps the first time in my life, I belonged to myself. My uncle had robbed me of more than my power; he had robbed me of my will. I had been like a child, drifting along, doing what I was told, lost in stories, my own strength a secret, even from me. But now I was determined and set on a course I had chosen, not one I was reading about and not one that had been chosen for me.

I was going to save my little brothers, or die trying.

The closer I got to Mattawa, the more I felt Colter's influence. The clarity and courage I had experienced on the bridge began to dissipate and tiny fingers of doubt tickled the back of my mind. *Did I really just have that conversation with Tia Donna? That was really crazy, wasn't it? All that talk about magic, boxes of memories? Uncle Oscar a magician? Me, a child of the goddess? Obviously, this was another paranoid delusion. Justin Colter was just a handsome guy. One I really wanted to see with his clothes off. That would be nice. After all, I'd felt his muscles. Naked, he would be...*

I slapped a hand across my face, letting the pain shock my mind back into focus. I realized that this is the way evil works. It turns your mind to trivial things, or sets it going in circles, so you don't move forward. With a great effort, I focused on my brothers, how much I loved them, how innocent they were, like great big dogs themselves, Fitz and Blob on two feet, kind and good hearted and fiercely loyal.

I thought of my brothers, of Xavier, and I drove that sputtering car to the orchards, to Uncle's groves, where I knew Colter would be waiting for me. The orchards were where I had lost myself in the first place. They were where I had given away my power. There, probably dozens of my uncle's charms still lingered. And like the little buried box I had dug up, Colter would, no doubt, use them to his advantage, to weaken me and make me turn away from myself, which was his intent.

He was waiting in front of my uncle's house, handsome as a dream. A full, midwinter moon shone down on his blond hair, spangling it with silver. All around him the snow-covered groves of trees glimmered. He looked beautiful and ghostly, his features clear and clean in the blue light of the moon, like an old time film star, everything shaded in crystalline white, stark black, dove gray.

I turned off the loud engine and slid from the car. Tia Donna had told me that he would try to rob me of my faith in myself, and since my sense of self was so unformed, I would be in constant danger of his lies. "The most difficult to remember is that he wants you for your power," she had said. "And that is what you cannot forget. That you are powerful."

And sure enough, as I lowered myself onto the snow-covered earth, I felt an immediate sense of helplessness. *He was a skinwalker. He might have been a man once, but he was so old and powerful now, I can never stand against him. Better to beg for his mercy. Better to offer myself to him now before he does something unspeakable.*

With a great exertion of will, I said, "Where are my brothers?" My voice sounded weak and faint in the winter air.

"Safe of course," said Colter. "I have no desire to hurt them." He held his hands in front of him, a gesture of innocence and invitation. "What's this Esmeralda? Are you angry with me? Come here, I can hardly see you in the dark."

I came forward and caught a whiff of his scent, Bay Rum and sage. I felt excitement flutter in my belly. *He was so damn handsome. Irresistible, really, when you looked at him.* I realized I was still wearing my dress from the memorial service. My legs were cold. I stepped forward again. *He could make me warm. He could put those big, warm hands on my thighs and fire me right up, I bet.*

I steadied myself with a deep, cold breath. I pushed the familiar, sexual throb aside. *It's just temptation.* Tia Donna had told me to ignore the innuendo, just cut to the chase. "The devil hates a direct approach," she had said.

"I understand you have a proposal for me," I said.

He laughed. It was a laugh of supreme confidence. He snapped his fingers and made a motion with his hands. Something heavy dropped at my feet. I kicked wildly at it, frightened at first. But I heard the clink of coins. "There's a fortune in that bag," he said. "Enough to set your brothers up for life. They could be mighty comfortable."

"And what do you get?"

"You, Esme. All of you. And what you can do."

"Why do you need it? Aren't you powerful?"

Something flickered across his face. "You're never rich or powerful enough, darling. If you'd lived as long as I have, you'd know that." He chuckled.

I set my teeth. "Oh, come on," I said. "It's not the money. It's not even the power, is it? It's because you can't make anything. Am I right? You traded your soul for riches and power, but without a soul you can't create, am I right? Creation is God's gift to us."

Colter spat, and I heard the snow at his feet hiss. "What a fool your uncle was." A hard edge had crept into his smooth voice. "Apples, for the love of Pete. He's got someone like you in his house and he grows apples. I've got a much better plan for what you have. Let's make a seed no one else can grow but us. Then let's make sure every farmer in the world has to buy it. Then let's control who can have it and who can't." His voice had gotten dark. "The man who controls the food controls the world. People might have forgotten that in the almighty computer age, but baby, everyone still has to eat, and you and I, you and I are going to see that they do. Eat it all up."

"So the winery is just a ruse?"

"Oh hell, we can make wine, too. Wine and wheat and whatever. Come on, Esme. Give me your hand, and I'll give you the world."

"I don't want the world," I said. "And you sound like some kind of cheap lounge lizard, Colter. I'll take my chances with someone else."

He didn't like that, I could tell. He grimaced and a little of his glamour fell away. Suddenly he didn't look that handsome anymore, and underneath the Bay Rum, I caught a whiff of something nasty.

"Have it your way, Esme," bitterness hardened his voice still more. "But I could make this so much more fun for us both." The moonlight caught his eyes as he looked at me, making them glow an unearthly, chilling white. "So you think you love him, is that it? But, you know, the thing is—" he grinned, and my skin contracted when I saw the flash of his teeth and that baleful silver light in his eyes "—I can keep him from you, Esme. I can keep your lover from you. And I will. If you don't give me what I want? I'll hunt him down the same way I hunted down your Uncle Oscar. You don't think I can?" He laughed, but it sounded more like a growl, deep in his throat. "I can hunt him down like a tiger, Esmeralda. And I'll tear him to pieces, sweetie pie."

"He's a powerful magician," I said.

"So was your uncle, believe me. And he screamed like a little girl in the end."

"He can fight you, Colter. He's not afraid of you."

Colter's voice dripped with contempt. "He's a son of Nanahuatzin, Esmeralda. Don't you remember your Mexican myths? He's not ruthless enough to stand up to me. He'll give of himself for the greater good or some crap like that. What did he do when your uncle tried to take you? He let you go. He sacrificed himself, because he didn't want you to hate him. Your Xavier. He might have all the power of the sun behind him, but in the end he'll give it away to save a falling sparrow."

His grin had grown wider, impossibly wide, so now it seemed to split his face as he spoke. His teeth were growing longer in his jaws and I felt my heart stutter in my chest as his voice deepened to a grinding rasp. "I took your brothers for his benefit, Esme," he growled as I watched, frozen by horror, as his body began to grow and distort right in front of my eyes. "Your Xavier's going to try to save those boys, and die as a hero, you'll see. He's on his way right now, all ready to do right by you. And he'll die, honey. Tonight or tomorrow doesn't matter. I'll see to it he doesn't live."

"Unless?" I choked.

"Unless you give yourself to me," he said, the words garbled in his huge, fanged mouth. "Give your power to me. Just say you're mine, and Xavier stays safe." He laughed, and the sound was terrifying, like gravel being flung into a deep hole. "You won't feel a thing, Esme. I promise, I'll make it quick. Shut your eyes. Shut your eyes and let me inside you. Soon enough, you won't remember, and I'll make it sweet, I promise."

Tia Donna had told me that the devil would speak in riddles, but somewhere in everything he said, there would be a grain of truth. And if I could find the truth in what he said, instead of believing the lies he told, I would hold onto myself. "The truth is the only freedom there is," she had said. "Stay true to yourself above all, Esme."

But this monstrous form made my mind split into a million pieces. I wanted to run and hide, scream and cower, do anything in the world but stand my ground. My legs turned to jelly, my teeth chattered in my head. The part of me that could ponder and reason about truth and lies had been eclipsed by another, stronger part of me, that simply wanted to run away, with a driving panic that was fast overtaking any other need I might have.

He has something you want.

The very sane voice that made itself heard in the turmoil inside of me was Tia Donna's, dark and bracing like a strong cup of bitter tea. I clutched the little spirit bag she had placed around my neck.

You have great power, Esmeralda.

I swallowed my fear. I clenched my fists. I looked at the monster. I said, "Xavier might die for me. He might die for my brothers. But that won't take him from me, Colter." I felt my voice getting stronger as I felt the truth of it. "The only way you can take him from me, is if you take away my soul. And you can't have it, Colter. You can't have it. Because I choose Xavier, whether he lives or dies. I choose him, as he is, exactly as he is, and in that choice, I take the risk of losing him."

And I quailed even as I said those words, for the monster sucked its breath in through its enormous fangs, and blew a stream of fire in my direction. I felt the heat blast as the trees around me crisped and burned and the snow melted in streams of dripping water.

And through the flames I heard the dogs barking. I knew help was on the way. They were coming, the people who loved me. They would die in a fire, every one of them, die defending me, if I didn't act quickly.

I heard the monster sucking in another great burbling breath, getting ready to blast another stream of heat and flame. Idly, I wondered why I wasn't burning. Hadn't he covered me with fire just a moment before? And then I heard Tia Donna's voice in my mind and she said, "Esme. The fire has no power over earth. Earth quenches fire, chica."

So I laughed at the monster as the fire washed over me. And I knelt and put my palm on the ground. Where my hand touched the earth, a great crack opened. And I watched as the earth swallowed up the Colter-thing, and my uncle's house, and a dozen blazing trees into the bargain. I heard the skinwalker howl with rage and fear as it fell in the pit, and my heart was moved by pity for a moment. But I set my teeth and slammed the hole shut and the ground shook beneath me with a roar like thunder.

25.

THE DEVIL AND HIS GARDEN PART 3

The Devil was pleased with Jardín as his slave, and he sat in his garden and enjoyed both her flowers and her unhappiness. He wiggled his scaly toes and ran his horny fingers down her hips and smiled his cold, cold smile.

But the Devil had overlooked one crucial thing. For though Jardín could coax trees and flowers to grow from the sand, she did not do it all alone. Her friend the Sun, who loved her with his whole heart, helped her with her work every day. He came and went over the walls of the garden, and every day, when the Devil's back was turned, he tried to remind Jardín abut who and where she was. "You don't belong to the Devil," he told her. "All he has put you through is an illusion, Jardín. You have all the power in this place," he whispered. "Climb the walls, Jardín and be free."

The Devil overheard the Sun talking to Jardín one day and became incensed. He said, "Come to me Jardín," in a terrible voice, and she came to him and the Sun was sad. The Devil laughed at the Sun. He banished him from his garden.

But without the Sun's light, all the flowers and trees promptly withered, and Jardín grew pale and wasted away. A cold wind blew all the leaves from the trees and frost petrified the ground.

Then the Devil grudgingly allowed the Sun back in, but he silenced his voice. He did not allow him to speak to Jardín and every time the Sun tried to, the Devil would say, "Come to me, Jardín," and the girl would drop what she was doing and sit by his side. The Devil would stroke her head and murmur his lies until she belonged only to him again.

But try as he might, the Devil could not stop the Sun from gazing at Jardín with love and respect, for the Devil has no power at all in the face of true love, he only knows hate and possession.

And slowly, slowly, day by day, Jardín felt the warmth of the sun on her skin, felt his fingers in her hair, felt his eyes on her face. And slowly, slowly, day by day, Jardín felt stronger and stronger. Until one day the Devil said, "Come to me Jardín," and Jardín said, "Why do I do what you say? Why do I give to you and you never give in return? What do I owe you, anyway?"

And she took the hand of the Sun and stepped over the Devil's wall forever. And without her, the Devil's garden withered to nothing. But she and the Sun made other gardens, elsewhere, and they were very happy.

26.

Seismologists will always be mystified by the earthquake that swallowed a house and half an acre of orchard on Midwinter's Day, in a place where there are no fault lines or volcanoes to be found. Astrologers blamed the Mayan calendar; geologists talked of a subterranean river, but a few of us knew it was really just one of Earth's daughters, sending an ancient monster back to hell, where he belonged.

Annie and Xavier, Fitz and Blob found me, shaking with exhaustion and reaction, blazing with a kind of spiritual fever, next to the new sink hole that used to be my uncle's house, holding a bag of gold in my shaking hands.

"I think I buried the Holy Terror," I said through shaking lips. "I'm sorry Annie."

"Did it fall on top of Colter?" she asked.

"You know, I think it did."

Fitzsimmons sniffed around the sinkhole, but didn't seem worried. So they bundled me into Annie's truck. And on the way home Annie got a phone call from my brothers, who had grown tired of waiting alone at Justin Colter's riverside mansion for someone to come get them, and wondered if they could hitch a ride back to the farm. So in short order, we were all safely together, and the sun rose that morning on a new year, and a new life, at least as far as I was concerned.

I tried to talk about everything that happened, and what needed to happen next, but Annie shushed me, and Xavier soothed me and right in the middle of it, Fluff decided to have her puppies, and the boys went crazy with excitement, so no one talked about anything important for quite some time. Suddenly every one of us remembered it was almost Christmas, that there was a bonfire and a party that night; there were gifts to wrap and songs to sing and love to celebrate and puppies to name. I won't say everything bad vanished in an instant, but everything good became clearer, and that was what we chose to focus on for quite some time.

Which is why, just a few hours after I'd battled a monster and made an earthquake happen, I was wearing a beautiful green dress, and sparkles in my hair, and Xavier was whirling me around at the Midwinter Fire Festival, and we had eyes only for each other. We danced until we were breathless, and then he took my hand and led me to the shadows, which was what I had been longing for. And he pressed his warm body to mine, and kissed me until I was dizzy, and I touched him in places that made him moan, and it was so good, so very good, so good I cried and then laughed and then cried some more.

"This is our story, you know," he said later, when we had slowed to small strokes and light touches and little kisses. We could see the bonfire faintly through the trees, but chose to stay apart, side by side on one of the bales of hay the Midwinter Fires committee had thoughtfully scattered throughout the party site, no doubt for amorous couples exactly like us.

"What is?" His body was so warm, I could never be cold while I was next to him, even on a winter's night.

His straightened up, pretending to lecture. "The sleeping princess is a symbol for the sleeping earth. The spell she is under is the chill of winter and the kiss of life." Here he kissed me, and I sighed with pleasure. "Is the kiss of the sun, who wakes her." He kissed me and began to stroke me again into some mindless, blissful place, but I held him away. "What?" he asked.

"I let you go," I whispered, my eyes suddenly swimming with tears. "That's how I beat Colter. He said he would kill you, Xavier, unless I gave myself to him. But I knew if I gave myself, I wouldn't have you anyway. So I let you go."

He looked at me and then reverently kissed my eyes and nose and lips. "Thank you, my love," he said. "You trusted me to fight for myself. You did me an honor. Would that I had trusted you the same way seven years ago."

"We really were just kids back then, Xavier," I whispered. "But not now."

He moaned. "Then why are we kissing in a hay stack like kids?"

I laughed. "Because I sleep in a bunkhouse with two brothers. Like a kid."

"What I would give for a bed and a week alone with you with no clothes," he murmured, plucking at my dress. "Like a grown up."

"We'll have that," I whispered.

"We'd better," he groaned.

❄

The police never solved my uncle's murder. Alex Sanchez followed up and questioned Xavier, but there was nothing at all to tie him to it, and he was quickly removed from the list of suspects. In time, the police released my uncle's body, and I laid it to rest in the earth. I do not know if my uncle rests easy, though. When I think of the way he kept me hidden from myself for so long, I feel deep anger. When I think how afraid he must have been in the end, I feel deeply sorry. Sometimes I am sure he meant to help me in the end, that he did not want me to become Colter's property, the way I had been his. Other times I know in my heart he was just weak and greedy, and he probably would have let me go. In the end, it doesn't matter. He is gone and all the wrongs he did have died with him.

I would have nothing to do with Colter's gold. Annie told me it could set me up for life, but I chose to bury it in Olstein's orchards. "Let it be a gift to someone who needs it more," I said. "Let Apple Tree Man decide who gets that treasure. I didn't earn it, and I don't want it."

Besides, I know I don't have to worry about gold; I don't need it to provide for my brothers or myself. I have the gifts of Xilonen. I can kindle the earth with my hands. I will always be able to feed us.

I can see my future clearly, see it for the first time in my life. How Annie will let me lease a part of her land. How out of that scrub I can grow fruit and lush fields. How Xavier's gifts can be harnessed in the summers to tame and direct the inevitable, healing wildfires that sweep the mountains. How he will build a house for us, with a big bed. How I will bear his children, who will always be protected by a succession of large, white dogs. How my brothers will grow to be fine, healthy, loving men, respectful of the earth and sky and everything in between. How the years will unfold in a wonderful circle, of love and rest and work and loss and love again, where none of us will cling and grasp and steal, but only take and give, in a gentle, ancient rhythm, as old as the dreams of the sleeping earth, waiting for her lover the sun to kiss her into waking again.

❄

About the Author

Elise Forier Edie is an author and playwright based in southern California. Recent works include the play "The Pink Unicorn," which performed at the United Solo Theatre Festival in New York, a short story, "Leonora," published in *Penumbra* magazine and several plays, included in the anthology "Original Middle School Scenes and Monologues," edited by Kent R. Brown. She is a member of the Authors Guild, the Romance Writers of America (RWA) and the Society of Children's Book Writers and Illustrators (SCBWI). She is married to actor Keith Edie. When she is not writing, she likes to make quilts and soup, but rarely at the same time. Please visit Elise at her website: www.eliseforieredie.com, Twitter @EliseForierEdie, Facebook https://www.facebook.com/EliseForierEdie

Questions and Topics for Discussion

1. Esme's Uncle Oscar used her powers for a seven-year term and provided a home for her and her brothers. Then he used her powers for another seven years, and gave her a college education and a car. Do you think this was a fair exchange? Why or why not?

2. Esme is angry when Xavier explains that he cannot save her from Justin Colter, but that she must save herself. Were you disappointed in him, too? How do you think their future relationship would differ if Xavier saved Esme, instead of insisting that she save herself?

3. Justin Colter has the power to change into a monster, but using brute force is not his main method of attack. How does he manipulate Esme into choosing what he wants? What traps does he create to lead her to him? Which characters in the book are immune to his influences? Why?

4. One of the messages of this book is that the chief weapon the devil wields is lying and tricking people into believing they are weak and alone; that the nature of evil has more to do with telling lies—frightening, paralyzing and distracting—and providing temptations, than it has to do with committing evil acts. Do you agree?

5. Esme is a student of folklore and fairytales, and fairytale motifs are threaded throughout the book, from many different traditions. What

are some of the fairy tales and/or folk stories used in *The Devil in Midwinter*?

6. An allegory is a story in which the characters and events depicted represent ideas or concepts. For instance, Xavier explains that the story of Sleeping Beauty is a kind of allegory for the seasons of the year—the Earth goes to sleep in the winter and is kissed awake by the Sun in the spring. It could be argued that *The Devil in Midwinter* is an allegory for growing up and claiming an identity. Explain how Esme's journey to her twenty-first birthday can be looked on as a metaphor for becoming an adult and accepting responsibility.

Other Myths & Fairy Tales Available from World Weaver Press

—

After Adam fell, God made Eve to protect the world.

Forged by Fate

(Fate of the Gods, Book One) a novel by Amalia Dillin

Adam has pursued Eve since the dawn of creation, intent on using her power to create a new world and make himself its God. Throughout history, Eve has thwarted him, determined to protect the world and all of creation. Unknown to her, the Norse god Thor has been sent by the Council of Gods to keep her from Adam's influence, and more, to protect the interests of the gods themselves. But this time, Adam is after something more than just Eve's power—he desires her too, body and soul, even if it means the destruction of the world. Eve cannot allow it, but as one generation melds into the next, she begins to wonder if Adam might be a man she could love.

Fate Forgotten

(Fate of the Gods, Book Two)

Beyond Fate

(Fate of the Gods, Book Three)

WOLVES AND WITCHES

A FAIRY TALE COLLECTION

Amanda C. Davis and Megan Engelhardt

Witches have stories too. So do mermaids, millers' daughters, princes (charming or otherwise), even big bad wolves. They may be a bit darker—fewer enchanted ball gowns, more iron shoes. Happily-ever-after? Depends on who you ask. In *Wolves and Witches*, sisters Amanda C. Davis and Megan Engelhardt weave sixteen stories and poems out of familiar fairy tales, letting them show their teeth.

"*Wolves and Witches* is a fabulous collection of re-imagined fairy tales. I made the mistake of starting it late one evening and couldn't go to sleep until I had read it all. With their dark prose and evocative poetry these sisters have done the Brothers Grimm proud."

—Rhonda Parrish, Niteblade Fantasy and Horror Magazine

"Dark and delicious revenge-filled tales! I Highly Recommend this fun and small collection of short stories."

—Fangs, Wands & Fairy Dust.

"Once I began to read this collection, I couldn't stop. Just as with those secretive princesses with their silken slippers gone to shreds, I danced among these pages until dawn!"

—Terrie Leigh Relf, *Illumen*

Beyond the Glass Slipper:

Ten Neglected Fairy Tales to Fall in Love With,

Introduction and annotations by Kate Wolford.

Some fairy tales everyone knows—these aren't those tales. These are tales of kings who get deposed and pigs who get married. These are ten tales, much neglected. Editor of *Enchanted Conversation: A Fairy Tale Magazine*, Kate Wolford, introduces and annotates each tale in a manner that won't leave novices of fairy tale studies lost in the woods to grandmother's house, yet with a depth of research and a delight in posing intriguing puzzles that will cause folklorists and savvy readers to find this collection a delicious new delicacy.

Beyond the Glass Slipper is about more than just reading fairy tales—it's about connecting to them. It's about thinking of the fairy tale as a precursor to *Saturday Night Live* as much as it is to any princess-movie franchise: the tales within these pages abound with outrageous spectacle and absurdist vignettes, ripe with humor that pokes fun at ourselves and our society.

Never stuffy or pedantic, Kate Wolford proves she's the college professor you always wish you had: smart, nurturing, and plugged into pop culture. Wolford invites us into a discussion of how these tales fit into our modern cinematic lives and connect the larger body of fairy tales, then asks—no, *insists*—that we create our own theories and connections. A thinking man's first step into an ocean of little known folklore.

Available in ebook and paperback.

Also from World Weaver Press

Shards of History
a New Adult fantasy novel
Only she knows the truth that can save her people.
Rebecca Roland

The King of Ash and Bones
A breathtaking four-story collection
Rebecca Roland

The Haunted Housewives of Allister, Alabama
Cleo Tidwell Paranormal Mystery, Book One
Who knew one gaudy Velvet Elvis could lead
to such a heap of haunted trouble?
Susan Abel Sullivan

The Weredog Whisperer
Cleo Tidwell Paranormal Mystery, Book Two
The Tidwells are supposed to be on spring break on the Florida Gulf Coast,
not up to their eyeballs in paranormal hijinks … again.
Susan Abel Sullivan

Cursed: Wickedly Fun Stories
"Quirky, clever, and just a little savage." —Lane Robins, critically
acclaimed author of MALEDICTE and KINGS AND ASSASSINS
Susan Abel Sullivan

Far Orbit: Speculative Space Adventures
Featuring Gregory Benford, Tracy Canfield, Eric Choi, David Wesley
Hill, and Others in addition to a Letter to SF by Elizabeth Bear
Science fictiction in the Grand Traditon—Anthology
Edited by Bascomb James

Legally Undead
Vampirachy, Book One—*Coming May 2014*
A reluctant vampire hunter, stalking New York City as only a scorned bride can.
Margo Bond Collins

Fae
Anthology of Faries
Coming June 2014
Edited by Rhonda Parrish

Ailen Ways
Darci Salazar Mystery, Book One—*Coming 2014*
The trick to working with drug-addled aliens is not to lose your head...
David J. Rank

Blood Chimera
Blood Chimera, Book One—*Coming 2014*
Some ransoms aren't meant to be paid.
Jenn Lyons

Virgin
Coming Fall 2014
Jenna Nelson

He Sees You When You're Sleeping
A Christmas Krampus anthology
Coming Holiday Season 2014
Edited by Kate Wolford

World Weaver Press
Publishing fantasy, paranormal, and science fiction.
We believe in great storytelling.

29635844R00089

Made in the USA
Charleston, SC
18 May 2014